EIGENOIDS
EPISODE 1

Aqua Quest

Kristine M. Palmer

PublishAmerica
Baltimore

First printing

Hardcover 978-1-4512-2775-8
Softcover 978-1-4512-2776-5
PAperback 978-1-4560-2284-6
PUBLISHED BY PUBLISHAMERICA, LLLP
www.publishamerica.com
Baltimore

Printed in the United States of America

Key Words

aquifer
crevice
evaporate
infiltrate
recycle
stalactite
stalagmite
Thunderhead
transformation

To Seth & Tyler-

May you always enjoy learning as an adventure.

"Discovering the world around you, Who knew it'd be such an adventure..."

Kristine Palmer

EIGENOIDS
EPISODE 1

Aqua Quest

Kristine M. Palmer

Set 2 50/70

PROLOGUE

It will be hard to believe me, I know. I find it hard to believe myself. In fact, if I were you, I'd consider either the fact that I am crazy or that you are crazy for believing me. Either way, no one else will believe the tale that I'm about to confide in you. Should you ever wish to share this wonderful discovery with anyone, you should be prepared—as I am—that seeing is believing. As you read these events, believe what you may, question what you dare, and above all—have faith that anything is possible when you believe.

Chapter 1: School's Out

I can still smell the papers and stinky gym socks like it was yesterday. With a crowd of fury, the hallways seemed to be a busy confusing network of classmates running to their lockers for the end of the year. The echo of the last bell was fading fast beneath the high-pitch screams of joy as I struggled to hear myself count all of my affects from my locker into my old, torn book bag. I was so glad to finally be getting rid of this childish book bag with a superhero on the front. Next year, my mom said I could pick out my own book bag since I was going into fifth grade.

"Say, Rye, see you at your birthday party! Can't wait! Catch you later, my dad is here. Bye," shouted my best friend, Scotty Pickers.

Scotty Pickers was about a year older than I was; but he always liked the things I liked. He was the brother I never had. I looked up to him because he had bright red hair and freckles. He was always getting teased about his gangly, skinny frame and geeky red hair. He was so strong and would never let it bother him.

When others teased him, he would say, "I am the way God made me. Too bad he didn't favor you like me and make you look special, too."

After that, what could anyone say? Most simply gave up and went away. One time, a bully took him so seriously that the bully ended up crying, thinking he missed something. He always made me laugh at myself, since, I too, was geeky looking. I had a short and stocky appearance, big ears, and was missing two front teeth for what seemed a lifetime of six months. Looking back, we were really tight. He, of all people, I thought would believe me. Strange how things turn out. He was actually the first person I told and the first to tease me and walk the other way.

"Can't wait either," I replied. "Have your mom drop you off early so we can hang out. Got to go, too. My mom is on her way. See ya."

Well, my mom showed up a couple minutes late, as usual. Her boss and traffic always seemed to keep her until the last minute. With all the confusion in the hallway, I managed to collect my end-of-the-year goodies and b-line it straight to the car in time to hear Mom embarrass me again.

"There's my little guy! Miss me? How was school? You are so big. I remember when I changed your diapers," she'd always say.

I hated it when she started talking about when I was in diapers, and so on. It was so embarrassing. I always tried to get into the car and get the door shut before my friends heard. I guess it was her way of letting me know that she missed me. To top it off, I was still stuck in a booster seat! I passed the age restriction for riding in a booster seat; but

I was still too short and underweight. Believe me, it is hard to be a big kid in school when you are still in a booster seat. This was the summer that I could ditch the booster. In fact, this was the last day for the uncomfortable, embarrassing kiddy seat. After this year, I was going to be a regular guy in the back seat touching the floorboard. I couldn't wait!

Boy, did I have plans for my summer, too. Since I was going into fifth grade, I figured I was big enough to stay at home alone when Mom and Dad were at work a couple of days a week. You see, my dad worked a split shift only a couple of days a week, at night. Mom worked during the week. A couple of days my dad needed to sleep during the day, so I could stay by myself while he slept, or so I thought. I planned to ride my bike, and go to the store and buy ice cream when I wanted. I also planned to have my buddy, Scotty, come over so we could play galaxy wars and army guys in the back yard all summer. I had already started planning my busy schedule when Mom interrupted my daydream.

"So, Rye, you anxious about Pa-Pa's next week," she asked while peering at me through the rearview mirror.

I could tell she had plans to foil my big summer. I could just see it now; the guys would never let me live it down. Ryan, a big guy needs a baby sitter? Are you kidding me? I had the galactic war of the century to defend and the soldiers geared up and ready to march on my command. Was I supposed to leave them because my parents were more scared then me to stay alone? I tried to protest silently, like I didn't hear her, in case she was just faking.

"Rye, did you hear my question? Pa-Pa is excited for next week. I guess he is planning activities for you guys to do together. Sounds like fun? You excited," Mom asked again.

She knew I was avoiding the subject. She always knew what I was up to before I even did anything. Some day I'll figure out how she knew. It just amazed me and yet, it stunk! No matter what I thought I knew, she knew it before I even sent a signal. Since I knew she wouldn't give up on the subject, I thought I'd try the big-boy tactic and maybe point out how much of a hassle the driving would be, in hopes of staying home.

"You know Mom, I am going into fifth grade next year, right," I slowly replied.

"Yes, I know. Dad and I are so proud of you," she said, peering over her sunglasses.

"Won't it be a hassle to drive me there and pick me up every day? He is far away you know. I could save you the trouble and stay at home when Dad sleeps. He'll be there. It's not like I'd be really alone," I said as I tried to quickly head her off from being a hovering mom.

"Now Rye, we talked about this already. You are going to Pa-Pa's a couple days a week, while Dad sleeps. If he is sleeping, he can't watch you. Besides, I know you are a big guy; but Pa-Pa needs the company, too. He isn't getting younger and you should spend time with him when you can. When he gets older and lives in a nursing home, you won't get to see him as often as you want. Someday he may be gone and then you'll miss him," she cautioned me.

Her response never allowed for a rebuttal. How could I argue over not seeing Pa-Pa? She was right that I'd miss him when he was gone. It isn't like I didn't want to see him. I just wanted to save the galaxy first. I figured I could come up with some story for my friends so the teasing wouldn't be bad. Giving up rather quickly, I replied with a sigh,

"Ok. I guess I can go. If I'm good, can I still have Scotty stay overnight," I asked, giving her a look that always melted her heart and made her give in.

"That's my guy. We'll see. Let's get home and unloaded your stuff from school. Dad's waiting to see you before he goes to work," Mom replied checking her car mirrors.

And with that, the galaxy was lost, the soldiers were captured and I began the summer that would change my life. All of this happened in a matter of minutes, but it seems as though it took a lifetime to be realized.

Chapter 2: Party Time

The smell of bacon went drifting down the single corridor to Ryan's nose. Turning his head slowly from under the warm and cozy comforter, he began stretching and trying to keep dreaming. After all, he was in the middle of a galactic war that needed his starfighter to win the advance. Fighting the bacon smell and the grumbling of his tummy, he woke to his cat pouncing on his feet at the end of the bed.

"Kitty! Come on it is Saturday. Let me sleep," Ryan uttered quietly so his mother would not know he was awake.

"Ryan, breakfast! Bacon is ready. Come on and let's get up, birthday boy," Ryan's mom yelled down the hall.

That's right, it was Ryan's 10th birthday. Ryan's mom had made his favorite—bacon and pancakes with hot maple syrup. It was already 9:30 in the morning and Ryan had to get ready for the party. His best friend, Scotty Pickers, was coming over and they had planned a galactic war to take place in Ryan's room.

"Oh, yeah! It is my BIRTHDAY! I almost forgot," Ryan said, quickly jumping out of bed.

You see, Ryan had a way of pretending he wasn't excited, even if he was, in hopes of tricking his parents to give him extra-special attention. Ryan got dressed in his favorite galaxy war shirt with matching sweatpants and ran to the kitchen. Kitty was trailing right behind him trying to catch the starfighter before he made it to the barstool at the kitchen counter.

Trying to be nice, but in a hurry to eat, Rye asked, "Where's the bacon?"

"Hold your horses, son. Mom is almost done cooking it. Did you make your bed," Dad asked, and smiled as if he had a big secret.

Ryan's dad had a way of sneaking things into Ryan's room for him to find later as a surprise. Through the years, on his birthday, Ryan had found toy figurines, cars, balls and his favorite sports-team shirts all hanging on the back of his door or in his bed under the covers. Ryan knew the routine and went running back down the hall on a fervent search for the latest goody to add to his collections.

"Dad, what did you sneak in there this time," Ryan's mother asked as if to scold Ryan's dad.

"Nothing too big. You know about the figurine," Dad replied, chuckling and almost choking on his orange juice.

No sooner did Ryan's dad smile and Ryan shouted from the hallway.

"Yes! I got it," Ryan said, running to the kitchen clutching the latest action figurine that he needed for his collection. "Thanks, Dad! You're the bestest ever!"

"Ok, breakfast is done. Let's eat. We have a lot to do before everyone gets here," Ryan's mom said, setting the hot plate of bacon in front of Ryan.

Ryan began to immediately grab for the bacon as usual.

"Ouch! It's hot," Ryan said, shaking his hand up and down to cool it.

"It is hot, I just took it off the stove, silly. You do this every time. Wait just a minute, then take a couple of pieces," cautioned his mom.

"Dad," Ryan began to speak while waiting for his hand to heal. "Can Scotty stay all night and go to Pa-Pa's house with me tomorrow? Please, if I'm good today at the party?"

"Ryan, I don't think Pa-Pa can handle both of you. He is getting a bit old you know. How about if Scotty stays all night tonight and we take him home in the morning before you go to Pa-Pa's," Dad replied looking over the top of his newspaper at Ryan. Ryan was busy playing with his new figurine in stead of eating.

"I won't be able to take him home before work, dear. Why not let him stay over another night," Ryan's mom replied, pouring the orange juice and giving a scowled look to Ryan who continued to play instead of eat.

"Please, Mom, it is MY birthday! I'll be good, see," Ryan said, beginning to eat everything as quickly as he could.

"OK, Let me talk to Pa-Pa first before Scotty comes. If it is okay with him, then we can ask Scotty's parents before he comes to the party so he can bring his stuff with him. But, you have to be good or the deal is off. Got it," Mom replied. She always gave in when Rye gave a smile and tried being good to please her. "I'll call Pa-Pa after we're done here."

"Ryan, after we're done, while Mom calls Pa-Pa, let's you and I put up the piñata for the party, ok," Ryan's dad said. Ryan's dad was always thinking ahead and enjoyed getting out of the house.

"Sure thing, Dad. I'm almost done. There. All done. Let's go. Don't forget to call Pa-Pa, Mom," Ryan mumbled quickly with food in his mouth on the way to the garage door with Dad at his heels.

Ryan's mom picked up the dirty dishes and cleared off the table. Grabbing a cup of coffee, she sat down and made the call to her father.

"Hello, Dad? Thought I'd give you a call before the party today for Ryan. He wants to have a friend come with him tomorrow over to your place. I thought I'd ask you before he put you on the spot over here in front of his friend. You remember Scotty, right. Well, he wanted him to come with him. Will that be ok? I won't have time to drop him off at home before I make it to your house on my way to work in the morning. He could stay tonight for Ryan's birthday and then come with him in the morning. I could bring him home later when I pick Ryan up. They could keep each other busy so it may be easier to watch Ryan. What do you think," Mom asked. Ryan had snuck back into the living room to overhear his mom talking on the phone.

"Yes, that's right. Scotty, the redhead. I can bring him home when I pick up Ryan," Mom said. Ryan's mom caught a glimpse of him peeking around the corner and tried to ignore him.

"I think they'd like that. That should keep them busy, I'm sure. Just don't work them too hard."

Ryan jumped in front of his mom after he heard the word, "work." That didn't sound like fun at all.

"Ok, thanks, Dad. I'll tell him. See you in a bit. I'll keep the event a secret so you can tell him. Love ya, bye," Mom said. Ryan's mom hung up the phone and saw a worried look on Ryan's face, as if he was going to have to do chores. Laughing at him, she smiled and bent over to give him a hug.

"It's all ok," Ryan's mom said. "Pa-Pa said, no problem. Scotty and you can both come together. In fact he has a surprise for you two. I can't tell, so don't ask. Go ahead and call Scotty and tell him to bring old clothes for tomorrow. You guys are going to have fun."

"Fun! Work? I heard part of what you said. Are you sure? Yeh - Scotty can stay! Boo on work," Ryan replied, not knowing if he should yell and jump around as usual, or be depressed and not invite his friend. How could he invite a friend to go play and then have him do work? Was his mom crazy?

"Ryan, not all work is boring and dull. Sometimes it is fun and creative. Scotty and you will have fun. Trust me, ok. Go call your friend and get ready for the party. Now let me get set-up, ok," she said. Ryan's mom had a way to make Ryan see the best in things.

Ryan called Scotty and had him bring old clothes for tomorrow. They made plans for the evening to watch their favorite movie and play galaxy wars all night. When he got off the phone, guests started to arrive for the party. Ryan hated greeting everyone as if he had not seen them in years. Actually, he spoke to almost all of the guests the day before, either at school or on the phone. Most of the guests were family, aunts, uncles, cousins and so on.

After all of the guests arrived, including Scotty, it was time for Ryan to blow out the candles on his birthday cake. Ryan's mom typically baked a cake, but this time she had a cake made with Ryan's favorite galaxy war hero on the top. Ryan was so surprised he couldn't blow out the candles. Finally, after two tries, he got all 10 blown out.

As his mom cut the cake, Ryan began to look at his presents.

"Can I please, Mom? Now," Ryan asked, trying to be patient.

"Ok, Dad can start handing them to you while I pass out the cake," Ryan's mom replied, laughing at how hard Ryan was trying to be good.

One by one, Ryan's dad brought the presents to him to open. He read each card and was sure to say thank you even if he didn't like what he received. Finally, after all of the presents were opened, Ryan realized that he hadn't opened one from his Pa-Pa. Pa-Pa always gave Ryan the best, most special gifts. One year, Ryan's Pa-Pa gave him an electric motorcycle. It was a Harley Davidson bike, only in small scale for kids. Last year, Ryan got a fishing pole and tackle box filled with lures and bobbers. He was anxious to see what he was going to get; he couldn't hold in his excitement anymore.

"Pa-Pa," Ryan said, climbing onto his grandpa's lap, "did you forget something?"

"Nope, I don't think so. You mean, you didn't get your special gift," Pa-Pa asked with a weird smile.

"I didn't get anything from you. Are you sure you didn't forget," Ryan asked. His mom gave him a stern look for asking.

Ryan's mom had a way of giving him a simple look and he knew he was in trouble. He knew he had better not ask grandpa again, or Scotty was not going to stay overnight.

Pa's. I'll want a full report," Ryan's dad said, giving him a hug good night.

"Love ya, Dad," Ryan said, jumping into bed.

"Goodnight, Mr. Wolf. Thanks for the game," Scotty said while snuggling up into his superhero sleeping bag beside Ryan's bed.

"Ok, lights out boys," Ryan's dad said, flipping off the lights and closing the door.

Ryan's dad made his way to the kitchen where mom was cleaning up from the party. She was putting the last dish in the dish drainer as Ryan's dad snuck up behind her.

"Down for the count. Good luck. Remember they are just boys. They'll probably be talking all night. I turned the lights off. But, I noticed Ryan's flashlight was on his nightstand and not his desk. Easy access I guess. I'll see you when I get up in the afternoon," Ryan's dad said softly to his mom as he gave her a hug from behind.

"Oh. No problem. He is such a good boy when he wants to be. They're excited about tomorrow, I'm sure. In fact, I'm still curious about my dad's present. You know how he is. I'll have to let you know what I find out," Ryan's mom said as she hung up her apron and towel on the stove handle.

"Now honey, don't worry about it. I'm sure it can't be too bad. Besides, most everything of importance he has already given to you and your brother and sisters when your mom passed away. Whatever it is can't be too important or harmful, to say the least. Have a good night and don't worry. You'll know when Ryan does," Ryan's dad said as he put his coat on and went to the door.

"Ok. Love you. Thanks for putting them to bed. I'll see you when I get home after work tomorrow," Ryan's mom spoke as she kissed Dad goodnight on the cheek.

Ryan's dad went out the door. Mom locked the door behind him and he gave it a couple of good rattles to make sure it locked tight. Mom turned out the lights and got ready for bed. Once she got her pajamas on and watched the late news, she heard the boys giggling. Down the hall she went to quiet them down and invade their galactic war which was going on in a heated battle.

"Ok, boys," Ryan's mom said as she swung open the door to catch the boys playing.

Ryan was faking being asleep under his covers with his head hidden. Scotty, too, was faking that was asleep. Mom, however, didn't fall for the trick. She saw the toy gun figurines hidden under Scotty's pillow and Ryan's blanket.

Slowly shutting the door behind her and standing really still, Ryan's mom acted as if she had left the room. Thinking she was gone, Ryan pulled down his comforter and turned on his flashlight. Scotty raised up and began to play like his gunfighter was shooting at Ryan's starfighter ship.

Turning on the closet light, Ryan's mom shouted, "Got ya! Come on now, boys. Lights out. The battle is over. You can finish this next time."

"Ok, but, it isn't a battle, Mom. It was a war," Ryan mumbled as he handed her the flashlight and crawled back into bed.

"Sorry Mrs. Wolf," Scotty answered as he snuggled back under the covers.

"It's ok, just go to bed. Don't forget, tomorrow is Pa-Pa's special gift you know. Now go to sleep," Ryan's mom said. She turned out the lights, shut the door and went back to her bedroom.

It took some time for Ryan to finally go to sleep. All he could do was dream of Pa-Pa's gift. Was it a bike? Could it be a BB gun? Whatever it was, Ryan could hardly stand the suspense. He knew it must be something his mom would not like. This made Ryan even more curious. He would have to wait until tomorrow. For now, all he could do was dream and hope that whatever he dreamed was a good guess.

Chapter 3: The Morning Arrival

Today was the day. The mystery gift would be revealed. Ryan and Scotty could not wait. Today, Ryan's mom had no problem getting the boys up, dressed and eating breakfast. In fact, the boys woke up early. The had gotten dressed and were sitting at the kitchen bar watching television, waiting on Ryan's mom when she came into the kitchen. She could hardly believe her eyes.

"Well, good morning, boys. How'd you sleep," she asked bending over to kiss Ryan on the head.

"Mom. I'm too big for that, now. Just good morning. Besides, I slept just fine. When are we going," Ryan replied, as if to hide the fact that he was anxious.

Ryan knew that if he was too anxious, his mom would start in about how she would need to know about the details with his visit at Pa-Pa's. Besides, Ryan didn't want her to worry about whatever the surprise was in case it was a BB gun. Ryan didn't want to have to lie.

"Now, Ryan, Scotty needs to eat his breakfast and so do you before we go. I need to finish getting ready for work as well. We'll leave in just a bit. Thanks for getting ready for me. I knew you could," Ryan's mom said, hurrying back to her room to finish getting ready.

"Scotty, what do you think it is," Ryan asked his cohort in crime.

"What are you asking me for? I have no idea. Besides, if it is a gun or bike, since I'm with you, you have to share, right? You know your Pa-Pa will come through. He always does. I wish I had a Pa-Pa like you do. Mine only gives me clothes or board games," Scotty replied, downing his orange juice.

"Yeah. I'll share. But, you keep it a secret if we are told to, Ok? He is pretty cool for a Pa-Pa," Ryan said, slapping Scotty on the back for approval and hopping down to tie his shoes. "Mom, we're ready when you are."

"Ok, get your shoes on. I'm ready, let's go," Ryan's mom said as she hustled back down the hall from her room.

Ryan had not only put his shoes on, but he and Scotty picked up the cereal bowls and juice glasses and stacked them in the sink for his mom. Seeing this, Ryan's Mom smiled and grabbed her purse.

"Thanks, Rye. Let's go."

Ryan's mom opened the door and away they went. Ryan and Scotty climbed into the back seat of the car with Ryan's mom in the driver's seat. In just a few minutes, Ryan would be at his Pa-Pa's house and the adventure would begin. He just didn't know how right he was.

Turning into the gravel driveway at Pa-Pa's house, the car made a crackling sound as gravel rolled under the tires. Ryan could see his Pa-Pa looking through the screen door as his mom pulled closer to the door.

Barely waiting for the car to stop, Ryan and Scotty jumped out and ran to the door.

"Ok, Mom," Ryan shouted to the car. "See you when you get back from work. Have a good day!"

"Ryan, come back here," his mom shouted back.

Ryan ran back to the car asking, "What?"

"I love you. Be good for Mom, Ok? Don't get into trouble. Tell Pa-Pa I'll be back around four o'clock," Ryan's mom said, leaning out of the window to speak to Ryan. "Now, get going."

Ryan ran back to his Pa-Pa and waved at his mom. She waved back as she put the car into reverse. Still wondering to herself about the gift, she trusted everything would be fine for a short time while she was at work. Truthfully, how could anything seriously go wrong.

"It'll be fine. They'll be fine," she told herself as she looked back at the three of them through the rearview mirror.

"Well, boys. I mean men. Are you ready? Let's get started shall we," Ryan's Pa-Pa said as he gave Ryan a hug and shook Scotty's hand.

"What are we doing? Are we going somewhere? Is it my surprise," Ryan couldn't wait. He began with a million questions to which Pa-Pa could only smile and nod.

"Maybe he didn't hear you, Rye," Scotty whispered to Ryan.

"Nope, I heard you," Ryan's Pa-Pa smiled down at the boys. "Let's get going shall we. Lot of things to do today."

Shrugging their shoulders at one another, Ryan and Scotty began to follow Pa-Pa through the house to a back bedroom. In the bedroom was a closet with a single light hanging with a string dangling from it. Ryan had only been in this room a couple of times. This was a guest bedroom for him to stay in if he stayed the night. Ever since his Grandma had passed away; however, the room became a storage area for all kinds of clutter. Ryan had never seen the closet or the strange steps heading up into the ceiling. They must lead to a secret room, so he thought. Ryan's Pa-Pa was always finding things and collecting odd items. A secret room wouldn't have surprised Ryan.

Chapter 4: Treasure Hunt

"Here we are men. I figured we could go through the attic and clean it. Never know what treasures you may find. The last time I was up there was before your mom was born, Ryan," Pa-Pa said as he straightened up the ladder, making sure it was secure. "Up we go, now."

"Awe Pa-Pa! You wouldn't? Are you sure? We have to do this? Why? What did we do that was bad? I did my chores for Mom this week," Ryan uttered, trying to be respectful.

"Come on Ryan, it might be fun. I helped my dad do this last month. When I was done, I got his rookie Sandberg baseball card I found. He's right, you never know what you can find," Scotty said, urging Ryan to go up the ladder.

"He's right Rye. Never know. Maybe I'll find something like your special present when we're done? I'll be up right behind you," Ryan's Pa-Pa said as he put his hand on Ryan's shoulder to help persuade him.

"You sure, Scotty? You don't mind? You don't want to play war instead," Ryan asked Scotty.

"Play war, huh. Is that what you guys do? You know I was in the war? The real war. Didn't seem funny to me. In fact, didn't seem like play at all," Pa-Pa tapped the steps on the ladder to summon Ryan up the ladder.

Climbing up the ladder, Scotty and Ryan began to be intrigued by the old man. Had he really been in a war? Why hadn't anyone ever told Ryan before? What was in the attic? Any war stuff? Ryan became very curious as he climbed into the dusty attic. Scotty too was getting anxious as to what they would find.

Once at the top, dust began to surround them. Coughing and covering their mouths, the boys began to swing their hands to try to clear the air. As the dust started to settle, Ryan and Scotty could hardly believe their eyes. With a small, dim light hanging above them, they began to focus on the room. To the left in front of them was a small air vent window. The sun shined through creating a stream of dust particles dancing in the rays. Amidst numerous boxes, there were a couple of trunks, old clothes hanging on headless mannequins. To their right was an old, cracked mirror hanging above a dresser. The mirror was shaded in such a way that a reflection was hard to see. Beneath their feet were a couple of old rugs on the old cracked, creaky floor.

"Cool," Scotty said coughing as he slowly began to move around peering at the different artifacts from years gone by.

"Wow, Pa-Pa, what a mess," Ryan said, then sneezed as he was turning around to see Pa-Pa coming up the ladder behind them.

"I know. Let it go for years, son. Was hoping you boys would help me clean it up while I was able to climb up the ladder. In exchange for your help, I'll let you keep something you find," Pa-Pa said as he came into the attic.

Pa-Pa knew all of his old Army stuff was up there from when he served in the war. Assuming the boys were typical boys, they would love to go through his old stuff. In addition, his most special gift for Ryan was buried somewhere in the attic. He was sure if Ryan found it, that it would be the treasure Ryan would ask to keep.

"So, where do we start," Ryan asked with a puzzled face.

"Why not start over here? Look," Scotty exclaimed as he ran over to the oldest looking trunk.

"No. Let's start on one corner and work our way around. I didn't realize there was this much stuff up here. I guess the fact that I am so old, things do have a way of piling up on you. I'm afraid this may take more than today to get through this stuff. Say, you guys are getting pretty old yourself. How about earning a bit of money this summer by staying with this until we get her done? How does five dollars a week sound," Pa-Pa asked the boys knowing they wouldn't turn down money.

"Really? You'll pay us? Both? Just to help clean this out? You got a deal, right Scotty? And can I still pick out a present to keep," asked Ryan.

"I'm in. Just need to make sure I can come help with my Mom," Scotty replied, nudging Ryan in agreement.

"Deal. Now let's get to it. Lunch will be here before you know it," Pa-Pa said with a grumbling stomach.

The three went to the closest corner and began to move things into the light to see. Pa-Pa assigned roles to each. Together they moved item into the light. Pa-Pa would sort the items. Scotty would be the one to put things in the discard pile. Ryan would put things into the keep pile. If either found something they wanted, they could ask to keep it for themselves, if Pa-Pa agreed. When they were all done, each could select one item to keep. With the ground rules in place and the duties assigned, they began to attack the piles. The jobs sounded pretty easy; however, easy does not mean speedy. Going through years of clutter and keepsakes also means unearthing a flood of memories and stories.

Pa-Pa would select an item from the center pile and either immediately give it to a sort pile or he would start to dwell upon it and really examine it. This reaction quickly became a clue for the boys to begin asking questions. Pa-Pa, of course, was a great storyteller and loved to share memories with the boys. He seemed like a child at Christmas.

At first the stories were boring to Ryan and Scotty. They dealt with relationships and sentimental events like first dates or minor trips to boring educational places. Looking pretty tired and hearing their stomach grumbles, the boys urged Pa-Pa to break for lunch.

"Pa-Pa, I'm a bit hungry and thirsty. Is it lunchtime yet," Ryan asked.

"I hope so," Scotty added as he shuffled his feet over to his pile with one last picture frame for his growing pile. "A lot of stuff in mine."

"Not as much as mine! Hey, I thought you were cleaning, Pa-Pa. We are not getting rid of too much stuff. Mom cleans and has hardly anything left. Maybe she could help you out," Ryan said with a laugh.

"Yes, it is harder than I thought. We'll get it done though, wont we boys? I am hungry, too. Let's break and go downstairs. I think I hear some hotdogs calling us," Pa-Pa said as he began to stand up from the old rocker he was sitting in. "This one is a keeper for sure." He patted the chair's arms in approval.

On the way to the kitchen, the boys stopped in the bathroom to wash up. Pa-Pa could tell they were getting tired and bored with the work; however, it needed to be done and they were going to get paid. He began to try to think of a way to get them more interested in the stuff upstairs. Maybe, he thought, we should go straight to one of the trunks. It could be like a buried treasure to them, he thought.

"Ryan," Scotty said in a whisper, "Are you having fun?"

"No," replied Ryan softly. "Mom said it would be fun today. It usually is. I'm sorry. Maybe we could ask to stop for today and come back tomorrow? Then we could play pirates or war or something until my mom gets here."

"Well, it would be more fun; but, we already said we'd help. Besides, I really want the money for a new galactic toy," Scotty said as he put the soap back on the dish and began rinsing his hands.

"Yeah, I guess you're right. I could use the money, too. Say, didn't lunch come quick, though? Maybe it went fast cause of all the stories? Let's see what other stories he can tell? Maybe we can get some good ones about the war stuff," Ryan said, reaching for the towel as if to race Scotty. "Last one to the kitchen is a pirate prisoner."

The boys ran down the hall racing to the kitchen. Laid before them was the best lunch they had ever set their eyes upon. To their amazement, Pa-Pa had fixed them hotdogs with ketchup on the side and cheddar cheese corn puffs. Each had a big glass of cherry Kool-Aid at the top of their place setting. This just happened to be their favorite thing to eat. Pa-Pa always knew exactly what they liked - always.

"Chow's on," Pa-Pa said in a gruff voice, clearing his throat.

Scotty and Ryan each looked at the other over the rim of their drinks.

"So, you boys having fun, yet? Come on, tell the truth, now," Pa-Pa seemed inquisitive of their conversation in the bathroom. Coughing, he continued, "I wouldn't blame you if you wanted to quit for the day. We could start over and play pirates. Maybe look for buried treasure?"

Ryan and Scotty both almost choked on their drinks. Had Pa-Pa read their minds? How could he possibly know what they had been thinking unless he had been listening in on their conversation?

"Well," Ryan started to speak, but Scotty frowned and gave him a slight kick under the edge of the counter. "To tell the truth, Pirates would be fun; but, we did say we'd help in the attic. Besides, there are a couple of galactic toys we need for our collection and we were planning on saving the money from work to buy them. How about we work just a bit more," Ryan said, trying to compromise while Scotty looked on.

"Yeah. Just a bit more," Scotty repeated as he reached for his ketchup-soaked hotdog.

"Ok. How about we pretend we are pirates this time and look for a treasure chest. After lunch we can work while we search for it under all the stuff. I've been thinking the good stuff might be in the trunk you pointed out with the lock on it. We can treat it like buried treasure. Then we can play and work at the same time. What do you think," Pa-Pa cleared his throat once more from the dust he had inhaled.

Both boys nodded as their mouths were full of hotdogs and cheese puffs.

"Aye, Aye Captain," they said, raising their cheesy fingers in a salute while mumbling,

The race was on to finish lunch and get back to a treasure hunt. Pa-Pa was now Captain Beard, named for his white beard of course. Ryan became known as Rough-Necked Rye, while Scotty took on the name of Serious Scotty. When lunch was finished, Pa-Pa put the dishes in the sink and gave each boy a handkerchief to tie on their heads like real pirates. He thought that would aid in the fun and they could use it to wipe their sweat since the attic was hot during mid afternoon.

Making their way back to the attic, Pa-Pa stopped at an old wooden desk. The desk had been made from hand-carved wood slats from a tree. According to the history passed down in Ryan's family, the tree came from the homestead of his great- great-great-grandfather's farm when they settled on the Dakota Territory. Ryan had heard the story many times. What was Pa-Pa looking for? He seemed to be searching through the desk in a fervent mess. Given the mysteries surrounding the desk, Ryan began to wonder about the trunk.

"Pa-Pa," Rye said, stopping himself. "Oh, sorry, Captain Beard. What ya' looking for matey?"

"Just the key. Well, I think the key," Pa-Pa replied. "This old desk is so old. I remembered that there was a small case that Grandma used to keep old keys in. I suspect one might be for the old trunk with the lock. We used to put old keys in a special case in this old desk so in case we ever ran into an old lock we might still have the key in stead of throwing it out."

"What if you don't find it," Scotty asked, peering down from the top of the attic stairs.

"Not to worry. We can always blow it up with gunpowder, right," Pa-Pa asked, jokingly. "Isn't that what pirates do?"

"Oh, Pa-Pa," Ryan said while bent over laughing.

"Bye George! Found it. Let's hope one opens the trunk," Pa-Pa said as he turned around, slapping Ryan on the back.

"Knew you could do it, Captain," Ryan shouted and started up the stairs.

It was official, the treasure hunt had started.

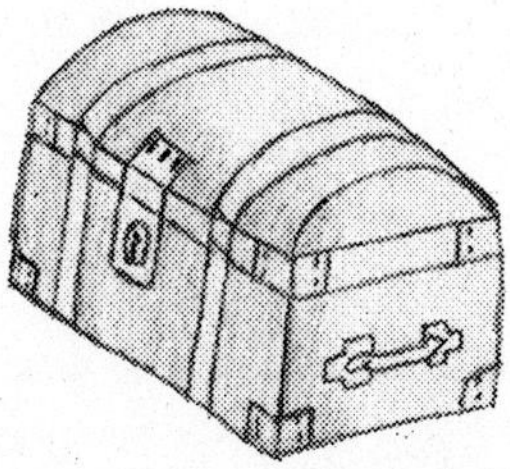

Chapter 5: X Marks the Spot

To begin the hunt, the pirates had to first clean their mess and take stock of their supplies. This meant that the boys had to straighten up their piles and make sure Pa-Pa agreed with what he had put in each one. Naturally, Pa-Pa had to change a couple of things and swap them from one pile to the other. Finally, they were ready to start the search for treasure. Little did they know they were really looking for something that was so priceless. Pa-Pa had suspected that the gift he was planning for Ryan might be in the trunk. Only time would tell. But, it began to be very obvious his suspicions were correct.

As the boys removed clutter of rags and old clothes from around and on top of the trunk, they found stuff from Pa-Pa's childhood. Now it was officially fun for the pirates to swab the deck, as Pa-Pa had put it.

Among the many items outside of the trunk was an old metal fire engine. It still had a working ladder that had chipped white paint on it. There was a half-rotted cord on a manual crank that when turned would raise the ladder and extend it. Ryan and Scotty couldn't believe their eyes. Pa-Pa played with cars and trucks just like they had a couple of years ago. In fact, every now and then, a good car race could be heard from Ryan's room as someone wiped out on a curve. The most astonished look came from Ryan when he found a small figurine stuck in the cab of the fire truck. It was an action figure of some kind that was dressed as a cowboy.

"Hey, Captain. Look what I found. A cowboy, " Ryan said, pulling the toy out and running over to Pa-Pa.

"Well, well. Good find, my matey," Pa-Pa said, peering over his glasses at the old figurine. "Lone Ranger. I thought I had lost you. That is the Lone Ranger. He was my favorite hero when I was a bit younger than yourself."

"I heard of him from my Pa-Pa," Scotty replied, looking up from a box of old magazines and comic books. "Isn't he like our super heroes are now?"

"Not exactly, but close. He always saved someone from some disaster or evil plot. In the end, he always road off into the sunset with his best friend, Tanto. I used to play with the Lone Ranger and my best friend had a Tanto figurine. Old Billy and I used to play for hours, like you guys play galaxy wars, so I'm told," Pa-Pa said, putting the figure in his shirt pocket for safekeeping. "Yep, this trunk must have special things in it if he was guarding it."

"Well, let's keep going," Ryan said, urging his Pa-Pa on. Finally they had the stuff cleared away and the boys tried to slide the trunk closer to Pa-Pa so he could open it.

"Oh, Captain," Scotty said, playing along with the names. "Rough-Necked Rye is too weak to move the trunk. Can you help us?"

"Who you calling weak, Serious Scott? I can take you any day," Ryan said, acting like he had a sword to fight Scotty.

"OK, men. No mutiny on my ship or I'll have you both swab the deck or walk a plank," Captain Beard replied, laughing. "Be right there."

Pa-Pa came over and the three of them began to go through the numerous keys. Pa-Pa tried a key. It didn't work, so he gave it to Ryan. He then tried another key and gave it to Scotty. After about four or five keys, Ryan and Scotty looked puzzled. If Pa-Pa didn't find the right key, what would they do to open the trunk?

"Well, only two keys left. Let's try them. Keep your fingers crossed. Not sure how to get her open if these don't work. We may have to keep looking, only for a key, not treasure," Pa-Pa said, keeping one finger crossed for luck.

"Nope, not it," replied Scotty.

"This has to be it," Ryan said, putting his hand on Pa-Pa's shoulder.

"Afraid not, son," Pa-Pa said, looking sad and puzzled.

Just then, he spied the old dresser in the opposite corner. He recognized it. The dresser had been his parent's when he was younger. That dresser had been passed down to him years ago, along with the trunk. Could the key really be in the dresser after all of these years? There was only one way to find out. Pa-Pa helped himself up with his cane and walked to the dresser. It was a tall, upright, narrow thing with small drawers on top. In fact, it was a writing dresser with compartments segregated for letters and pens or pencils on top. The top actually had a hinged front so someone could open the top and fold it down to write on a desk surface. Inside were more compartments for storage. Pa-Pa reached inside and removed a piece of wood from one of the compartments. It was a secret drawer of some kind. Ryan and Scotty looked in amazement.

"Wow, still here. Let's try this one," Pa-Pa said, turning around.

He was holding a rather large, funny looking key. The key looked like something from a medieval knight's era. It was dull and heavy looking. It just had to fit, Ryan thought.

"Try it Captain, Try it," the boys shouted with excitement.

"I remember now. You see, that dresser was my parent's and then it became mine. As I grew older, I used to hide things in that secret drawer. This is the key for sure. Ready, men? Her she goes," Pa-Pa replied with excitement, hoping that the special gift was inside.

With a slow poke of the key into the slot and a grinding turn, the lock opened. Pa-Pa and the boys raised the lid and let it drop to the back of the trunk with a loud thud. Dust flew up, but they didn't mind. After all, the treasure was about to be theirs. Inside of the old, tattered trunk were remnants of the degraded leather straps from the lid. They had apparently been tossed inside to keep with the trunk or some strange reason. The paper liner inside of the trunk was peeling off and had fallen from the lid onto the contents. This was really shaping up to be an expedition and search for what lied inside.

"Any clue what's inside," asked Ryan as he peered at the yellowed, gritty paper pieces.

"Money," Scotty asked. "You know, buried treasure, right? Coins?"

"Well, if that is in here, we are rich for sure," Pa-Pa replied coughing vigorously due to the dust. "Let's look."

They began to slowly lift the gritty paper out of the trunk and were amazed at what they could see underneath. Beneath the paper were what looked like antique school supplies of some kind and old clothes. There was a child's Army P-Coat overcoat and small goulashes. Wrapped in an old handkerchief was a tin cup with a metal spoon. Underneath that was a miniature chalk board and a half-broken piece of chalk. In addition, there were a couple of thin books. Both were thin, had brittle yellowed pages, and torn bindings. Stuffed in the corner was a folder with some children's papers and handwriting pages.

Ryan and Scotty looked through the contents in awe. This stuff looked really, really old. In fact, it looked too old to have been used by Pa-Pa. Some of it looked like it came from the pioneers. Pa-Pa was too young for that, Ryan thought.

"Pa-Pa, whose is this stuff," Ryan asked. "It came from the pioneers?"

"Well, some of it was your Great-Pa-Pa's and some of it was mine. You see, I lived in a small rural town. There was just one schoolhouse with one room. All the grades went to school in one room at one school. There weren't different schools, different classes and different teachers. There was one teacher who taught all grades together. My family was poor so I had to pack my lunch in this cloth sack. Our town was poor and we didn't have new books every year like you do. The younger kids used the books from the older kids when they were done, so, the books got torn up pretty bad by the time you got them. Paper was a luxury when I was in first grade. I had to learn to write on this chalkboard. It wasn't until I hit fifth grade or so that the school could afford paper. Yep, you guys have come along way."

"Wow. Really. You had all grades in one room? You mean, I would have to sit and hear a teacher teach ABC's even though I knew them and was in fourth grade? You're kidding, right," Scotty asked.

"Yep. You would of course be doing your assignments in reading and trying not to pay attention until your turn came," Pa-Pa replied, wiping his eyes with his handkerchief.

"I didn't know all that," Ryan said. "Mom told me you used to be poor and only had one pair of shoes a year for school. She didn't say anything about not having paper to write on, or the other stuff. I always thought she was teasing me so I wouldn't ask for basketball shoes."

Laughing at Ryan, Pa-Pa put his hand on his shoulder, "Rye," he said looking at the innocent little boy with a dirty face and pirate handkerchief on his head. "When you are young, you don't realize you are poor or wealthy. You just depend on your parents to provide and accept things the way they are. Only after you grow up do you realize how the world works and the cost of things. I didn't know I was poor. I knew we didn't have much, so I took good care of things my parents gave me. This is why you see I have so many things from my childhood stored up here. I took care of things because I didn't get new things all of the time. I also wanted to save the things that were important to me because they became my pirate treasure over the years."

"Captain, you are the best," Rye replied and stretched up to give his Pa-Pa a big hug.

"Say, what's this," Scotty said as he leaned over the trunk reaching for a flap on the lower side.

"Don't know, Serious. Pull the tab and find out," Pa-Pa said looking with a curious eye over his glasses.

"What," Rye asked.

"It looks like a trap door of some kind inside of the trunk," Scotty said, pulling the tab as a flap came open.

"Oh, my," Pa-Pa exclaimed.

"What is it? What is it," Rye shouted as he pushed Scotty over a bit to see for himself. "Pa-Pa?"

"Well, I'll be. You see, my Mom, your great-Grandma, packed this trunk for me when I went off to the Army. She told me she filled it with my childhood things and I could have it when I got older. Well, when I got married and went on my own, I took possession of the trunk but never really opened it other than to look just inside the top. Seeing the stuff on top, I never went any farther. I guess she packed some stuff I never knew about. Let's see what there is? I didn't know about the trap door."

"Hey, look, a note," Ryan said, pulling out a yellowed piece of paper.

"Read it Captain," Scotty urged with an intent look.

"Ok," Pa-Pa said, taking the note from Ryan and reading out loud:

"To my boy, I placed this in a safe place for you. Here is your treasure box that Pa-Pa Joe gave you.

I hope you remember this and the fun adventures you used to make believe with him on the farm.

When you outgrew the make-believe adventures, I placed this in your trunk for safekeeping.

I hope it brings back memories as you have a family of your own. Maybe you can find your

childhood as you play those fun stories over with your children. Love, Mom."

"Scotty, my boy. You found it. I was hoping it was in here. I was disappointed when we didn't find it, but you did! You found the treasure," Pa-Pa said, slapping Scotty on his back and becoming as excited as a child seeing Santa at Christmas.

"I did," Scotty asked, looking surprised.

"Uh, Pa-Pa. There is only a pile of rags," Ryan said as he reached down to pull out the torn bits of cloth.

To the boy's amazement, they felt something inside. Pulling the clothes slowly to unwrap their jewels, they found what appeared to be a wooden box with a small symbol carved in the top.

"That's it. I remember it. It was there! Ryan, bring it here," Pa-Pa said now seated in the rocker and patting his lap. "You come too, Serious Scotty."

The boys, looking very puzzled, went to the old man sitting in the rocker. The light had moved through the window so that it now shown brightly on Pa-Pa's face. Ryan could see tears in his Pa-Pa's eyes and wondered what was so special about a wooden box.

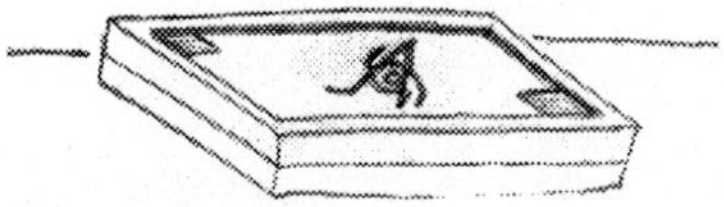

Chapter 6: The Box

Pa-Pa looked at his watch to check the time. He wanted to make sure he had enough time for what he was about to do before Ryan's mom picked them up.

"It is only 1:30 p.m. Good. We found it in time," Pa-Pa said.

"In time," Ryan asked. "In time for what?"

"Well, your adventure of course," Pa-Pa replied, sounding a bit confused—or so the boys thought. "Try to open it, Rye. Go on, try."

Ryan began to pull the lid from the bottom, but was having no success. No matter how hard he tried, the tighter it seemed to become.

"I can't," Ryan replied with a frown on his face. He continued to struggle as best as he could, putting all of his force and might into it. It was no use. "It is a trick, it doesn't open."

"Let me try, " said Scotty, reaching for the box.

Pa-Pa laughed and let them try. Neither could open it. Finally, after two or three attempts, he took the box back.

"Nope, it opens. Believe me. It opens. Before I open it, I have a story to tell you about how we became the guardians of the box. Ryan, this is the present I want you to have. I am getting older and it needs to be passed on and protected. It was up here all of these years and I regret my children not having it. But, it should go to you, if you are chosen. Make yourselves comfortable and have a seat."

Ryan and Scotty did as the old man asked. Pa-Pa had never really taken a serious tone like this before, so the boys were going to listen and do as they were told. They were thinking that he was getting ready to tell some wild story, and they were up for some more tales.

"According to the story, we don't really know the time or exact place. But, a long, long time ago, a young man went to war. Now this was so long ago, it was before there was even a United States or even the continent of America had been discovered. Maybe even when there were knights and dragons. According to the tale, like I said, a young man went to war," Pa-Pa spoke, leaning back in the rocker.

"War? Knights and dragons? Seriously, Pa-Pa," Ryan interrupted.

"Now, come on, just believe the tale I'm telling. You need to or you won't be chosen," Pa-Pa replied and then continued to tell his story. "So, this man went to war for his country. They were invading a small village that had threatened to harbor the enemy. His troop began torching every house or hut that they came to. Women and children were running for their lives. The men of the town were being put into chains and made into slaves to help his army. Now, the young, man didn't believe in hurting anyone. He especially didn't like to fight. He tried to lag behind his troop so he wouldn't be in the main fight. He only stuck someone if they were attacking him. He couldn't raid the towns as his troop did. He was noble, honorable and kind. Well, he came to a hut with an elderly man crouched beside it. The old gentleman seemed of some importance, by the way he was dressed. He cried for help, but the troops ignored him. He was too old to be a slave so they were leaving him to die. He begged the young man to come help him, so he did. He could not leave him injured on the ground. When he went over, he heard a small cough from inside of the hut. A small child was inside the burning hut. Acting as quick as he could, the man jumped into the burning hut. Inside, he found a small boy under a bed, coughing and scared. He grabbed the child and made it out of the hut just before it collapsed. The old man and child embraced for joy that he had been saved. By now, the troop had left the village and was on their way to the next town. The young man decided to stay in the town to help those that his troop had hurt. It ended up that the old man was the town teacher and spiritual leader. The child the young man saved was the old man's grandchild."

"Like, I am yours, right," Ryan interrupted.

"Shush," Scotty scolded Ryan.

"Yes," Pa-Pa continued. "In fact, the old man was so thankful that he gave this very box to the young man. It contained a secret that only one who believes can open. It has passed down from generation to generation in our family. My Grandfather gave it to me, and now, I am giving it to you."

"What am I to believe in?" asked Ryan.

"Well, I don't know how to explain it, really. I think you are to believe all things are possible and all things are good. You see, as a person grows older, they tend to change what they believe in, or how they look at things. For example, you trust that you will have supper this evening, right," Pa-Pa asked Ryan and Scotty.

"Of course. I'm having meatloaf," Scotty interjected.

"Yeah, I'm having soup," Ryan replied.

"Well, that is because your parents are planning to cook it for you. You don't need to worry about if you are going to have it, as children you just know you will be fed. You don't have to see it or smell it right now to know it will be there. Your parents, on the other hand, worry about dinner and what to feed you. It is their responsibility, not yours. They have to be sure to make enough money to buy the food and be able to prepare it in time for you to eat it when you are hungry. See the difference—kind of?"

"Sort of," Ryan replied. "Is it like what we learn in church? You know, that guy, Jesus. We can't see him, but he was real. He did stuff for us and all we need to do is believe he did them. He did the worrying and paying the bills for us. All we did was believe he did and know he was there?"

"So, what is so special about the box?" Scotty asked Pa-Pa to continue.

"Well, yes, the box. Ok. You see, it is starting to come back to me. The box is handed down in the family. Only a person who believes can open it. It contains special creatures called Eigenoids. They are very small. So small in fact, that you need a magnifying glass to see them. There should be one in the cloth. I kept it with it all the time," Pa-Pa could tell the boys were beginning to laugh at him until they saw the spy glass just as he had said.

"Ryan, look," Scotty said.

"Is this it," Ryan asked, handing a small, black-handled magnifying glass to his Pa-Pa. "What are Eigenoids?"

"Well, I'll get to that in a minute. The old man who gave the box to the soldier showed him the secret to unlock the box. There is a saying and special tricks to open it. I hope I can remember. You see, he was a teacher. He used the Eigenoids, these special creatures, to help teach to his students. He believed they were spiritual creatures who could do magical things to his students to help them learn. Boy, I used to spend hours with them. I don't think they'd recognize me, today. You see, as I grew older, my beliefs changed and soon I could no longer open their world. That is when I stopped opening the box. One day, I went to open it to see my friends and it was locked. It has been locked all these years. They know who believes and can chose who they will invite to open it. Once you have been chosen, you can open it for as long as you believe in their magic,"

"Ok, now you're scaring us. What do they do? How do they help us learn things," Ryan asked and scooted closer to Scotty.

Scotty scooted closer to Ryan, "Let's not open it right now. Maybe tomorrow or the next day, right?"

"Oh, I can't open it. I have to try to remember how and Ryan must open it. You want to, don't you? Remember, they were my friends and friends of your relatives going back for years. You know those adventures that my mom mentioned in her letter. They were not make believe. They really happened. Adults couldn't believe, so they said that I pretended to go places and do things. They never believed I was telling the truth. They are friendly. You believe, don't you," Pa-Pa said, asking the key question.

This all seemed far-fetched for Ryan and Scotty to grasp. Here was his Pa-Pa, an adult, telling them of a magical world and strange creatures that helped him with schoolwork and learn different things. Ryan reached for the box and Pa-Pa handed it to him willingly. The symbol on the top seemed very old and chipped. The wood seemed dry and cracked. It could be very old in deed. Pa-Pa's story was told with an almost serious tone. He wasn't joking as he usually did. Maybe he was telling the truth. It couldn't hurt to trust his Pa-Pa. With a long silent stare, Ryan began to rub the box lid.

"Let's try it out. What do I do, Pa-Pa? You sure it is safe? They won't try to hurt us because they don't know us, will they," Ryan asked in a shaky voice.

"Oh, Ryan. You believe, don't you? Let's see," Pa-Pa said, sitting up on the edge of the rocker and rubbing his chin in deep thought.

Scotty moved back from Ryan to give him room. Ryan took the spyglass and got on his knees. He placed the box and glass side by side on the floor in front of himself. Pa-Pa leaned way over.

"Let's see. If I remember, place your thumb on this corner. Put your finger on this one. Now, repeat the following verse and push in on the symbol when you say it. The symbol will sink into the top of the box and a latch will pop out from the side. You can lift the latch if they let you. Ready," Pa-Pa asked Ryan.

"I guess so," Ryan replied with a hesitant voice.

"Ok, I remember it like it was yesterday. Repeat after me:

A true friend I'd like to be, let me believe before I see.

Looking at the world about, teach me to see from the inside out.

Ryan repeated the phrase and shut his eyes to concentrate really hard. He really wanted to open the box and see these magical creatures he now believed existed. Scotty looked in utter amazement as the box appeared to get deformed and a latch appeared as Pa-Pa had said.

"Ryan, look! Open your eyes! It is working! The latch! You did it," Scotty shouted.

Ryan looked down, and to his surprise, the latch had appeared just as Pa-Pa said. The only thing now was to see if he had been chosen to open the box. Ryan got up and placed the box on a table directly in the light to see what would happen next. Pa-Pa grabbed the spyglass and Scotty joined him. The three were ready to open the box.

Suddenly from the bottom of the attic stairs came Ryan's mother's voice in a hurried tone.

"Boys. Ryan, Scotty! Aren't you about ready? We need to get Scotty home. It is getting late. You need me to come up and help tidy up for tonight," Ryan's mom said, starting up the stairs.

"Oh no, Mom. We're coming. Just a minute," Ryan shouted back.

Before they could say another word, Pa-Pa had taken the box and spy glass and wrapped them up in the cloth as they had been found. He started to tuck them under his shirt so they wouldn't be seen.

"We'll be right there. No need to come up, we're on our way down," Pa-Pa replied as he hid the box. "That was close boys. We can open it next time. Let's not keep her waiting."

Pa-Pa assured the boys in a calm manner and moved them towards the ladder. As Ryan and Scotty started down the stairs, Ryan looked back and saw his Pa-Pa rub the box and the latch disappear. He quickly put it back in the cloth and placed it under a blanket for safekeeping. He looked as if he was hiding a treasure.

Strangely, though, he waved goodbye to the box and whispered something to it like he was talking to someone.

"But, Pa-Pa, what about," Ryan began to ask, but, Pa-Pa stopped him in mid-sentence.

"That is ok. We can finish up tomorrow, right boys," Pa-Pa interjected.

"Well, Ryan can," Mom replied. "Scotty, your mom said you were going out of town tomorrow and would be gone for about a week to your cousin's. If they are not done by then, you can come back to help."

The boys said good bye to Pa-Pa and headed towards the car.

In a quiet voice, Scotty began to talk to Ryan, "Well, that was fun in all, but really, can you believe your Pa-Pa. He really thought he had us going for a minute on the trick box he had. You didn't believe all that stuff he was telling us, did you?"

Ryan didn't quite know what to say. He actually believed his Pa-Pa. After all, why would he make such a story up in front of Ryan's friend if it weren't true? Ryan had seen him talking to the box, which was rather odd.

How could he confide in Scotty that there really could be some truth to what his Pa-Pa was saying, if Scotty was going to act that way?

"Well, don't you think it could be. I mean, what if it was true? Wouldn't it be awesome? I'm not sure," Ryan replied in a softer voice so his Mom wouldn't hear their conversation.

"You can't be serious. Little creatures? If they take you let me know. Are you sure you are old enough for fifth grade next year? You seem like a preschooler. I tell my sister things like this and she believes me," Scotty said, laughing at Ryan and scolding him.

"I guess you are right. Pa-Pa does like to tell stories. After all, we did pretend to be pirates all afternoon. Let's forget it," Ryan said as he buckled up in the back seat.

"Forget about what," Ryan's Mom asked.

"Oh, nothing," Ryan replied as he nudged Scotty. "Let's finish our galaxy war."

With the boys buckled in their seats, Ryan's Mom backed out the gravel driveway. They were on their way to drop Scotty off at his house and then head home. As they drove, Mom tried to get information from the boys to no avail. All Ryan would say is that Pa-Pa had promised them they could select something from the attic and give them five dollars each for helping him clean. They hadn't found what they wanted to keep yet. It wasn't long before they had reached Scotty's house. Ryan and Scotty parted ways and Scotty ran inside his house waving back to Ryan as they drove away.

Ryan's house was across town and they had a ways to go before they got home. On the way, Ryan began to wonder about Pa-Pa's box. Was it really true, or was he making it up? He knew that he had told his Pa-Pa that he believed him. He didn't want to change his mind. After a long agonizing thought on the way home, he decided to believe in Pa-Pa's story. What could it hurt, he figured. If it was true and something did happen, he could tell Scotty and then he would believe also, or so he thought.

Once they got home, Ryan and his Mom washed up and the family ate diner. Ryan played ball with his dad as the nightly schedule went. This time, Ryan went to bed early so he could be rested for another day at his Pa-Pa's house. He had told his parents about playing pirates and could not wait to go exploring in the attic. Happy to see Ryan so interested in helping Pa-Pa, Ryan's mom and dad bid him goodnight, tucked him in bed and turned out the lights.

Ryan, of course, could not sleep. He pretended pretty well. However, thoughts of the box kept him awake most of the night. What would happen tomorrow? What were the creatures like? Could he really get to see them? Where would they take him? Thousands of questions and happy thoughts filled his head as he tried to sleep. Before long, he was dreaming of a peaceful land full of happy creatures and friendly smiles. He could hardly wait to have his adventure.

Chapter 7: Greetings

The night stretched on forever, so it seemed. Pa-Pa was looking out of the front window as Ryan's car pulled into the driveway. Ryan hopped out in a hurry and ran to the door to meet his Pa-Pa who, like him, had been anxiously waiting for this day. With a brief wave and smile from Pa-Pa, he and Ryan went inside and the day began.

"Well, you excited my boy," asked Pa-Pa as he looked down and placed his hand on Ryan's shoulder. "I have some friends I've been dying to see and want you to meet."

"Are you sure, Pa-Pa? I'm a bit scared. What if they don't like me? What if they take me away and I never get back? What if," Ryan had begun to almost shake in his voice.

"Oh, Rye. They aren't like that at all. You'll see. I love you and want you to have this special gift. I wouldn't hurt you or let anything happen to you. You don't have to go anywhere or do anything if you don't want to. I just want you to meet them and help take care of them. It is up to you," Pa-Pa assured Ryan in a comforting voice. I really miss them, now that I remember them. I hope they remember me since I have gotten pretty old from when we last spoke. In fact, I was just a couple of years older than you are when the magic stopped for me. It doesn't last, you know. Remember, too, it will have to be our secret. No one will believe you and Scotty about these creatures."

"Well, about Scotty. He doesn't think you were telling the truth. He thinks it is just a trick box. He doesn't think the creatures are real," Ryan muttered back.

"Oh, that is too bad, Ryan. He is your best friend. You know, it happened the same for me. I lost my best friend because he didn't believe me either. Maybe Scotty will come around. If not, don't be surprised. Remember, not everyone can have courage to believe before they see. Some never can. You'll love this, come on, cheer up. You are making five new friends for life who will never let you down," Pa-Pa assured Ryan and they went into the kitchen.

There, in the sunlight was the spyglass and the cloth-wrapped box. Pa-Pa had laid them on the table and had them all ready. Next to the box was a small leather journal. Ryan hadn't seen it before. He didn't remember finding it when he was there the other day. What an odd book. What did it have to do with the box?

"Pa-Pa, what's this," Ryan asked, looking puzzled as he began fumbling through the tattered pages.

"Why, that's my long-lost journal from my adventures," Pa-Pa replied as if he was bragging.

"Your adventures," Ryan questioned.

"Yes, my adventures. You see, after the first couple of times I went places, I thought I should write the adventures down. In here are all the places I went along with thing I saw and did. I figured it could be a guide book if I ever went to the same place twice. It helped a coupled of times because I had a tendency to forget minor things like paths and tricks, etc. I found it tucked next to the box in the trunk. We must have missed it yesterday when we found my box. I thought you may want to look at it and use it in case you decided to take any trips, you know, in case," Pa-Pa told Ryan as he sat down next to him at the table.

"If you say so," Ryan said. He seemed a bit reluctant to try to open the box, but he agreed to try.

Ryan pulled his chair closer to the table where the box had been placed for him.

"Ok, let's try it again. What is it I say,' Ryan asked.

"Well, place your hand the way I showed you. Remember," Pa-Pa said, leaning into Ryan.

"Like this?"

"Yep. Now repeat after me…

A true friend I'd like to be, let me believe before I see.
Looking at the world about, teach me to see from the inside out.

Ryan repeated the phrase and looked down. Again, the latch had appeared just as Pa-Pa said. The only thing now was to see if he had been chosen to open the box.

"It's ok, Rye my boy. Here we go. Take a deep breath and press down on the latch. When you do say:

With courage and faith to believe, will you choose me?

Ryan did as he was told and suddenly the latch opened. Ryan jumped back and was startled to see the box open on it's own. Suddenly he heard little laughs and voices. The voices were very soft and he could not make out exactly what was being said. A small ball of light appeared and seemed to float from inside of the box and rest on the table in front of him. The light was a rainbow of colors with a bright yellow glowing center.

Ryan sat and stared. He rubbed his eyes in amazement. He thought he believed, but he didn't know exactly how much he believed until he saw the light.

Pa-Pa began to laugh and slapped Ryan on his back.

"You did it. I knew you could. Congratulations! Boy I missed you guys," Pa-Pa said in an excited voice.

Pa-Pa could hardly stay seated. Ryan was frozen, not knowing what to expect. Pa-Pa picked up the spyglass and raised it to look at the light that was starting to dim. What was he looking at? Ryan saw what looked like dust where the light had been.

"Hello old friends. Man I've missed you. I hope you remember me. It's me, George. George Brandt. I know I've aged a lot since we last played. I was 13 then. Now I am 75. This is my grandson, Ryan," Pa-Pa said to the dust. "What's that, you say, you do remember me? What happened to me? No, I wasn't mad at you. I grew up and my beliefs changed. I couldn't open the box one day, and my Mom took it away. Remember, she never believed me about you guys. She put the box away. I lost you and couldn't get to you. I hope you have been ok. You look great! You haven't aged a bit like me. I'm really sorry.

Man, I missed you. I never got to thank you. You were my truest friends. Thank you for the memories. I'll cherish them always."

The dust moved a bit all on it's own and Ryan backed up in fear. He was still stunned and shocked at what he was seeing. Pa-Pa was talking to something, five somethings to be exact. Ryan couldn't make out what they were because they were so small. He could barely hear them and had to listen closely to see if he could make out their voices.

"Yes, this is he. You chose him to open the box. I couldn't, but he did. He is 10 and likes sports. He also plays galactic wars and likes pirates. Yes, it is just him. The other boy couldn't come today. Let me get a cloth and wipe his ears so he can hear you. Then you can talk to him and introduce yourselves. He is a bit scared, you know. This being the first he has ever seen Eigenoids and all. He is friendly and curious like I was. I know you'll hit it off. Just a minute," Pa-Pa continued talking to the dust.

Pa-Pa took a napkin from the holder on the table and wiped the inside of the wooden box. A strange residue glowed and deposited on the napkin. He then raised it towards Ryan's ear. Ryan, of course, backed away in fear.

"Wait! Oh, no you don't. You're not putting that weird stuff in my ears. No way," Ryan yelled and backed up against the wall in fear.

"Ryan, don't worry. It is magic and will disappear when it touches your skin. Your ears won't glow or feel a thing. You can't hear the Eigenoids unless you have had your ears opened by their magic. I was told this by my Pa-Pa. It works. Why do you think I can hear them and you can't? Now hold still. You only need to do this the first time you are introduced. It lasts as long as you can see them. Ready? It tickles," Pa-Pa said, walking over to Ryan and giving him a hug to reassure him.

Ryan agreed and grabbed Pa-Pa's hand. He squeezed it tightly and smiled.

"Ok, if you say so. I don't want blue glowing ears, though. Go ahead," Ryan replied.

"There. All done. Now let's see if you can hear. Come closer and let me introduce you guys," Pa-Pa said. He had wiped the film on Ryan's ears and they approached the table.

Very clearly, in a distinctive small voice, Ryan could hear little voices talking and carrying on about his Pa-Pa's looks. The voices were laughing and playing until he came closer to the table. Suddenly they stopped.

"Uh, oops, what's wrong? Did I do something wrong? Why'd they quit talking," Ryan asked.

"Now, guys, there is nothing to be afraid of. Ryan is a good boy. He will become a true friend if you let him. Go ahead. He can hear you, you know. Introduce yourselves," Pa-Pa said, scooting Ryan a bit closer and standing next to him. "Here you go, Ryan. Take a look."

Pa-Pa handed Ryan the spyglass. Slowly looking down into the dust on the table, Ryan saw the Eigenoids for the first time. He couldn't believe his eyes. Standing before him was five little creatures. Each creature was similar in form to a person except they were too small to be people. They each had a round head that came to a point like an onion. Their arms were long and skinny, and so were their legs. Although they all tended to look alike, each was unique in their own way.

"Uh, hello..." Ryan muttered as he stumbled to find a word to say. He was so stunned he could hardly speak.

Laughing at him, the first creature replied, "Hi. My name is Albert."

Albert was the leader of the group as far as Ryan could tell, since he spoke first. Albert wore glasses and had funny soft spikes protruding from his head like messy hair or a mop. His voice seemed to be a moderate pitch from what Ryan could tell. His skin had a blue cast to it and he wore a dark blue vest with matching shorts. Tucked behind one ear looked like a writing utensil, almost like a pencil.

"Let me introduce ourselves, Ryan. My Name is Albert. I am a mathematician and physicist," Albert said, pointing to the creature next to him on his left. "This is Newt. He, too is a physicist."

Newt was greenish in color. He wore a dark green vest with shorts and had similar spikes, except his were laying flat down on his head. He did not wear glasses, but he had a single spyglass tucked in his vest pocket. He pulled it out and raised it to his eye when he was introduced.

"Next we have Curie. She is a chemist. She keeps us in line," Albert said, pointing to another creature.

"Pleased to meet you. I hope you are as much fun as your Grandfather," Curie replied with a curtsy.

Now, Curie seemed rather frail in stature, but one could tell she could hold her own. Her skin was yellow in color and she wore a bright yellow dress. Her spikes were split into two pony-tails, one on each side of her head.

"Hey, don't forget me! I'm Vini. I'm an inventor. Anytime you need a bridge or machine, call on me," shouted a smaller voice than the others.

Stepping out from behind Curie came a smaller creature. He was reddish in hue and wore a red vest and matching shorts. Around his neck hung a round dial of some kind. Like Newt, his spikes were lying down on his head. He was the shortest of the five.

"Ok, Vini, my turn. I'm Louis. I like biology and chemistry. So, what types of things interest you, young man? Do you like school," Louis asked rather inquisitively.

He seemed to be the chubbiest of the five. He looked almost purple in color with a purple vest and shorts.

"Now, guys. He may not want to go on a trip right away," Pa-pa interrupted. "I just want you to meet him and find out about each other. I gave him my journal. You remember my journal, right?"

"That's fine," Curie replied, twisting her ponytail with her thin fingers. "You just take your time. We aren't going anywhere until you need us. It will be nice to have a friend in your realm again."

"My, realm? Where are you guys from? I've never seen anything or anyone like you before. Exactly what are you guys," Ryan replied, squinting harder to look through the spyglass.

"Didn't your Grandfather tell you? We are Eigenoids. We come from your world, but on the smaller scale where most people can't see us or hear us. In fact, you have been chosen to be our protector. You keep us safe and in turn we will help you learn the truth about the world around you. Since we are so small, we can go places you normally can't," Newt said.

All remaining four Eigenoids looked at Newt in amazement.

"What's wrong. I can speak. Just haven't felt like it much since George left," Newt replied.

"Oh, Newt. I missed you so much, too. I'm glad you are here for Rye," Pa-pa spoke with a shaky voice. "Well, I hate to break this up and be all sentimental, but Rye's Mom, my daughter is on her way by now and we need to get you guys back."

"Oh, Pa-pa, must they go? We are just getting to know each other, please," Ryan said, grabbing Pa-pa's arm.

"Your Grandfather's right, Ryan. Your Mom can't see us, and she might brush us off the table into the garbage as regular dust. Let's say good bye for now. Next time that you need us or want to talk, just say the phrase and we'll let you open the box," Albert said as the creatures all joined hands.

Slowly they nodded and waved good bye. Together they formed a circle and bowed their heads. As they moved in a rotary motion, they spun into a ball of light and drifted back into the box. Just as the box had opened, it closed and the latch disappeared.

"Pa-pa, your journal. Can I take it home to read? I want to read where you went. Maybe I can go the same places, or investigate where you went. I really want to read it. Can I," Ryan asked, pleading with his Grandpa.

"Well, I don't know, Ryan. Maybe you should leave the box here with the journal. Remember, can't tell Mom or anyone about the Eigenoids. No one will believe you. If you leave it here, I can help keep it safe until you need them," Grandpa said. He started to change his mind about letting Ryan take the box. He realized that he could be putting Ryan in danger.

"Oh, come on Pa-Pa. You said that I could have the box if I could believe and take care of them. You can trust me. You did when you were my age. Please, Pa-Pa? Please," Ryan begged his Pa-Pa with a crooked face.

"Ryan, I understand this all sounds great and I said I wouldn't hurt you. It has all come back to me now. Most of the travels they took me on were fun; however, some were fun and turned dangerous. A couple of times I needed their help to escape and return. If I give this to you, you must promise me you will be careful and only go to the places I marked in the journal that were safe. You must always carry the journal with you because it will help you find your way. Promise," Pa-Pa replied, looking down at Ryan with tears in his eyes.

"I promise. I'll be careful. Please," Ryan said.

"Ok, just remember what I've said. Here. Guard it with your most special possessions. Never let it out of site and you will pass it on to your children some day," Pa-Pa said, placing the box and journal into Ryan's hands. "Don't forget the spyglass, you'll need it, too."

Just then, perfect timing as usual, Ryan's Mom drove into the driveway. With a loud honk of the car's horn, Ryan said good bye to Pa-pa until next week.

"Love you Pa-Pa. I'll take care of it. See ya next week," he shouted as he ran to the car.

"What ya got, Rye," Mom asked as he climbed into the backseat with his hands full of his treasure.

Pa-pa raised his hand and waved good bye to Ryan and his friends. Wiping his face, he turned back and closed the door.

"Just my present," replied Ryan, tucking the spyglass into his backpack.

"Oh," asked Mom. "Well, what it is?"

"Uh, just a box and an old story book that Pa-Pa had when he was a boy. He gave it to me to read and put things in," Ryan replied, trying not to look too interested in it for fear that his Mom would ask to see it.

"Don't you like it," Mom asked. "You don't seem too excited. You know, Pa-Pa can't afford too much now that he is on retirement."

"I know. It is pretty cool. I'll put it in my room when I get home," Ryan said, putting the box in his backpack as well.

"I only worked half the day today. Let's go out for supper tonight. How's pizza sound?"

"That sounds cool," Ryan replied as he started thumbing through the old journal he had.

He must have worn himself out today, thought Ryan's Mom. Ryan was quiet the rest of the way home. He seemed really engrossed in the book. Mom didn't care since Ryan was reading and that was a good thing.

Chapter 8: The Transformation

Before Ryan's Mom could pull the car to a stop in the garage, Ryan was ready to jump out and head to his room with his treasure.

"Slow down. Let me at least come to a stop, silly. Where's the fire," Mom shouted at Ryan.

"Oh nothing. Just wanted to put things away in my room. Still on the cleaning streak, I guess. I'll be in there for a bit. Need some privacy, you know, Ok," Ryan said, running into the house and shutting the door behind him.

Ryan's Mom couldn't get out of the car fast enough before Ryan was in the house, in his room and had his door shut.

"Ok, as long as you empty your book bag and put stuff away. We're going to get a new bag before school next year, remember. No need to have that old thing laying around," Ryan's Mom yelled back to remind him.

"No," shouted Ryan. "I mean, I like it. Can I keep it for the summer? It can be my carry pack for things when I go to Pa-Pa's or on vacation. We can get one later. Please," replied Ryan through his door as he clutched the bag tightly with the box inside.

"It's up to you. Sounds fine to me. Just clean it out and all your school stuff, too. I'll be in the kitchen taking care of last night's dishes. If you want a cookie or snack, let me know. Love you," Ryan's Mom said. She seemed puzzled by Ryan's behavior.

"Ok. Thanks Mom. Love you, too," Ryan said as he moved from his door and placed the pack on his bed. This will make a cool backpack to travel with, Ryan thought.

Ryan quickly began moving stuff off of his bed and off of his desk. He wanted plenty of room to pack for his journey. He hadn't decided if and when he'd go, but he wanted to be prepared, just in case. He first wanted to get to know the Eigenoids. He was very curious since he had been reading his Pa-Pa's journal all the way home. Curiosity was gnawing at him; yet, he was scared and cautious to open the box.

At first, Ryan placed the box, the journal and the spyglass on his desk. After he placed them there, he backed away and stared at them for a bit. Where could he keep them so they would be safe? He didn't want his Mom to find them, or move them. At first he checked under his bed. That didn't work. Ryan remembered that his Mom cleaned his room a couple of weeks ago and removed old toys from under his bed. They ended up going to the school for the daycare and other children to play with since Ryan didn't play with them anymore. He couldn't let that happen.

Just then, Ryan spied his trunk at the end of his bed. Printed on the trunk in big letters was the word "PRIVATE." This was a trunk that Ryan's Pa-Pa had

made for him to put his keepsakes in. Rya looked in it, and inside Ryan kept his priz Inside were action figures and old toy woo He even had a favorite stuffed animal he with every once in awhile that no one kn would pull the animal out to keep him c rained and he was alone sleeping. It wa security. Mom would never look in t surmised.

Now that he had a hiding place, he decided journal and read a bit in the beginning to see a he wanted to go. When he opened the journa folded piece of paper fell out.

"What's this," Ryan asked himself, looking "I didn't notice this before."

Ryan unfolded the brittle paper and began to was the phrase he needed to repeat to open the written down. It had been written with a weird looked crooked and jittery in the wording as if a q had written it. Ryan guessed that it was the paper that came with the box. There were add phrases on the reverse side. Apparently, the phrase needed to be spoken to end a journey were inscrib

To go home, now that you have roamed, repeat the p below:

Now that I've learned to see, please send me back to wh should be.

Further inscription read a list of things to bring your journey for a safe trip. Listed in modern writi were the following: cookies, juice, pen or penci

shlight, scissors, string and a cap. Ryan thought that list was rather odd, but it must be needed. So, he set t to pack his bag for a trip. He grabbed the flashlight m his bed and string from a kite kit in his closet. Since hadn't fully unpacked his bag from school, he had a ncil and scissors already packed, so he left them in his ag. Next, he went down the hall to the kitchen to his Iom.

"Mom, I'll have that cookie, now. Can I have a couple nd a juice box, too," Ryan asked nicely.

"Sure, you working up a thirst in there," Ryan's Mom said, giving him an inquisitive look.

"Yep, can I take it to my room. I have a lot left to do before Dad gets home from the store," Ryan replied.

"Well, I don't like food in your room, but you are bigger. Ok. Don't make a mess and bring me the plate when you are done. Here you go," Ryan's Mom said, handing him a plate with three cookies and a juice box.

"Thanks, Mom. I'll be careful. See you in a bit," Ryan said, walking in a fast pace back to his room. He didn't want to run and cause his Mom concern, but he was anxious to open the box again.

Ryan placed the goodies on his desk and closed his bedroom door. He began checking his supplies.

"Box, journal, spyglass, food, juice, flashlight, pencils, string, scissors and a ball cap. All here, check," Ryan said to himself as he placed the packed bag on his bed.

Pulling the journal and paper back out along with the spyglass and box, Ryan sat on the floor by his bed.

Slowly he started to place his hands on the box and begin repeating the phrase written on the paper to open the box.

A true friend I'd like to be, let me believe before I see.

Looking at the world about, teach me to see from the inside out.

Just as before, the box opened and out came a ball of light. The Eigenoids were back. Ryan had opened the box all by himself. The ball of light traveled next to the box and landed on the carpet. Suddenly, small voices began to giggle and speak.

"Wow, so this is your room, huh," asked Albert. "Cool. Lots of stuff to explore."

"Well, hello again, Ryan," called Curie. She seemed bashful this time.

"Uh, Hi. Yes, this is my room. You guys will be safe here," Ryan replied, trying to be friendly and reassuring.

"So, I bet you have some questions huh," asked Newt, peering through his one eyeglass as if he was smarter than the group.

"Now, Newt! Give him time to focus. We are small and hard to see, remember. This is all new. Don't scare him off," Albert warned Newt in a scolding voice.

"I'm not scared. Should I be," asked Ryan.

"Yep, should be - I mean will be later," Louis quietly muttered in a soft voice so Ryan could barely hear him.

"Louis," Albert interjected to stop him from speaking.

"What'd he say? I couldn't hear him. He needs to speak up a bit for me," Ryan said.

"Oh, nothing important. Anyway, let's finish telling you about us, ok," asked Albert to change the subject quickly.

He proceeded to explain what Eigenoids were and their history.

Before the history of mankind - many worlds ago - Eigenoids were little beings that once inhabited the Earth and the universe. At one time, several worlds existed together, the Outer Realms, Animal Kingdoms and the Inner Realm. It was in this Inner Realm that Eigenoids ruled. A huge war took place and the Eigenoid king had the royal sorcerer shrink the entire Inner Realm and it's subjects so small that the other worlds could not see them to destroy them in battle. It was the greatest spell ever cast. It is obvious to mankind that humans think they won that war. In fact, that is quite contrary to the truth.

"So, have you ever wondered what makes your world work," asked Albert, taking a break from the history lesson.

"What do you mean," asked Ryan, who was quite engrossed in the story of the battle.

"You know. Ever wonder why a baseball player throws a ball and sometimes it is a strike, sometimes it is a curve or a slider? Ever wonder why a plant grows, or why electricity turns on a light," Newt said, interrupting.

"Well, not really. I never really thought about it. I guess, now that you mentioned it, yes, I guess I could wonder why and how things are the way they are for me," Ryan replied in an inquisitive way.

"Eigenoids," Vini shouted. "It's us, I mean, not us, here us—but, Eigenoids. You see, we do it."

"Ok, let me finish. You see, when our king shrunk our world, we then saved our world to exist at the same time as your world does. In fact, we took over the Inner Realm and everything we do affects your world. You could say that we won the war since it is because of us that your world exists the way it does. From our world, you can see and hear everything in yours, except from the inner view," Albert continued.

"So, why are you in a box? Why do I need to protect you," Ryan asked.

"Not long after our king, King Omnibus, rescued our world, his kingdom was overthrown by his ruthless brother, King Odious. As a punishment, we were sent to this box. Many centuries have past. We have since met your kind and found that human children are trustworthy and can help keep us safe from their adults who may seek to destroy us. In addition, by traveling in disguise to our world, we can visit our remaining friends and family without getting caught. You see, few are left that are loyal to our king. Most that survived the wars and the overthrow follow his brother," Albert continued.

"Yuck! King Odious. Now he is scary. He has spiky hair like Albert, but they are hard spikes. The front two have little twists on the ends like a bull's horn. And his color! Woo. Can't tell exactly. It changes from head to toe in a color array of red to orange like fire. Believe it or not, he even has one red eye. Story has it that a spear poked him, but his eye didn't explode. It just turned red with his blood and never healed. He can still see out of it and uses it to stare at his victims before he kills them. Mean to the core that one, for sure," Newt spoke up with his input to the history lesson.

"Wow. What a story. I promise to keep you safe. You can count on me," Ryan replied, shocked at the history he had just heard. He could hardly take it in when Louis began to lead the topic again.

"So, Ryan, is it, right? I see you just finished school, huh," Louis asked.

"Yep. Going to be in fifth grade next year," Ryan boasted proudly.

"Guys, let's see if Ryan wants to come visit our world, now. My neck is hurting from looking up so much," Curie spoke softly as she rubbed her neck. "Ryan, can you come over to our world to visit more down here?"

"How," asked Ryan. His curiosity was killing him.

"I know, let's visit the water cycle! He has a book on it right over there. Did you study about it in school," Louis asked, nudging Albert and pointing to the pile of books Ryan had laid at the foot of his bed.

"What? Visit the water cycle? Are you kidding or something? Yes, I did study it in school, but I don't recall anything about a water cycle in Grandpa's journal. I know he mentioned strange places like a city of weird cells inside of plants. He didn't mention water. Sounds ok, though. I know how to swim. Can't be gone too long or my Mom will worry. She thinks I'm cleaning my room so I can't go too far. So, how's this work," Ryan leaned over to ask.

"Well, ok. The water cycle it is. Ryan, grab your journal and pack. All ready," Albert asked.

"Ready, I guess," Ryan replied.

Suddenly as they appeared, the Eigenoids joined hands. They began to hum a quaint little tune and spin in a circle. As they went faster and faster, they began to rise off the ground and turn into a ball of light. When the light floated above Ryan he felt all tingly inside. He then began to giggle and saw the room get bigger and bigger. He was shrinking! Before he knew it, he was as small as the Eigenoids. Suddenly, after a quick glimpse of his room, he was transported into a strange dark area.

"Hey! Guys! Albert, Newt? Where are you? This isn't funny. I want to go home! I'm scared," Ryan said, clutching his backpack tightly and holding his journal close to his chest.

"We're here. You're not alone. Focus your eyes," Albert said.

"It's ok, Ryan. You're small like us," Curie replied and she reached out and grabbed Ryan's hand to assure him.

"Huh? Ok," Ryan said. He squinted, rubbed his eyes and then he could see them.

He was amazed. They all looked like water drops. They had turned into drops of water that were big, slushy and funny shaped. Looking down, he saw Curie's cold wet hand on his. His hand was also squishy looking like jelly, but a clear cloudy blue haze surrounded it.

"What happened," Ryan cried.

"We turned you into a water drop. You still have all of your stuff, right," Albert asked.

"Yes, it didn't change. It looks the same, only small. You mean, I am like water now," Ryan asked as he felt his body.

"Nope, not like water - you are a water drop," Louis replied as he splashed about.

"Too cool," Ryan replied. "I could like this. Where are we? Why is it so dark?

"Unfortunately, I don't know where we are," Albert mumbled. "You see, I never get this one right. I never know where it starts, so I can't control where we begin. I'm sure we'll figure it out soon. We can look for the start as we get going."

"Not again! In all this time, you still haven't figured out where it starts," Newt scolded Albert.

"Say, you have the journal, right," Vini said. "I'll bet it's in there somewhere. Let's look and find out where we are."

"Find out quick. I don't like it here. It is dark, slimy and I'm beginning to stick to the floor," Ryan said, grabbing the journal from his pack and handing it to Albert.

"Ok, let's look," Albert said, opening the journal and turning pages in a mad hurry. "I think I've found it. No, that's not it. I need a light."

"Here," Ryan said, grabbing his flashlight and passing it to Albert.

"Newt, hold it for me," Albert said, passing it to Newt.

"Now let's see," Albert began again.

Chapter 9: Slimed

Before Albert could finish his thought, Curie exclaimed, “Oh, gross! You’ve got to be kidding me!”

“What is it,” they all shouted and turned around to have Newt shine the light on Curie.

“What’s that on your head,” asked Ryan.

“I don’t know, but it stinks and is slimy. It is dripping off of the walls. Can we please get out of here? I’m starting to absorb the gunk around me,” she cried.

Ryan looked and saw Curie with a piece of something floating inside of her stomach. He then realized that the longer they stayed there, the dirtier they would become and the more they would literally soak into their surroundings, the way water actually does.

“Hurry, we are sinking or soaking into the gunk,” Ryan yelled.

“Rats! It isn’t in here,” Albert replied.

“What do you mean, not in there,” asked Ryan in a panic. “I thought Grandpa wrote down everything and everywhere he went with you guys. It has to be there.”

“Almost everything. You see sometimes he forgot the book, or was too busy to write stuff down. That is why it was an adventure every time. Some stuff was recorded, others not so much. Anyway, I don't remember this in the water cycle. And I've traveled this enough to know," Albert explained calmly.

"Apparently you don't know as much as you think you do," replied Newt sarcastically.

"Hold on, Curie, we'll get out of this," Vini assured all of them as he began to squish up and down to look around.

"What are you doing," Ryan asked Vini.

"I'm thinking. Actually, I see a light up there and I'm trying to see where it goes. I also see a thing sticking up in the middle of the room. I'm trying to move over to it to get a closer look," Vini replied. "Can you help me roll closer to it?"

"That's my boy, Vini. You can figure this one out," Newt replied.

"Looks mechanical of some kind. Wow, it has a knife blade stuck to this bolt! It is a torture chamber," Vini yelled.

"A what," Ryan exclaimed. "Wait a minute! Who would torture water? And with a knife? Get real. Think about it. Slime, stinky, wet, gross, mechanical knife, water - I know where we are. I can't believe it, but I know where we are."

"Ok, smarty. Where are we? And what is this place," Albert smirked back with a hurt ego.

"We're in a garbage disposal in a sink," Ryan replied proudly.

"A what, where," asked Curie.

"You know, a garbage disposal. Garbage gets put in here before it gets ground up and washed down the drain in a sink," Ryan began to explain calmly.

"Garbage, ground up and washed away! Let's find our way out before we get ground up," shouted Albert.

"You're right. I hadn't thought of that. What will we do," Ryan began to cry.

Just then the motor starter to hum.

"Quick, everyone grab hands and sit on top of a knife blade. Hold on as tight as you can until our water friends join us from the faucet. If we stay on the blades until the rest of the water gets here, we can go out with them and not get cut by the blades. We can ride them until it is safe! Hurry," Vini replied, jumping on a blade and holding his hand out to Ryan.

Vini was the mechanical expert of the group. He was always figuring out how things work or run to evaluate them. Whenever the group would get in a bind, Vini would figure a way out of tight situations. They always followed his advice when he came up with a plan. As usual, he wasn't wrong. By sitting on the blades, they easily escaped getting cut or mixed into the slime and garbage stuck to the sides of the wall. When the water filled the room, they jumped off together and swam about until they found a way out through a pipe opening.

"Hold on everyone, here we go! We made it! Everyone safe," shouted Albert and Curie.

Ryan was swimming for everything he had. He had always been a good swimmer, but the current was stronger than he had ever faced in real life. He was falling behind when he saw the motor start to slow and a door to the exit pipe start to close. It was the valve on the disposal. The others had passed it no problem; however, Ryan was falling behind and running out of time to clear the valve. Stretching for all he could, he made his way to the edge of the opening. Suddenly he saw his pack and journal floating. He stretched back and barely grabbed the strap on his backpack.

"Got it," Ryan sputtered out of breath. "Wait for me! I just need the journal!"

"No! Ryan, you'll be stuck or squished in two pieces! Leave it! Please," Curie screamed above the sound of the motor pulling on Ryan's arm to yank him through the pipe opening.

Suddenly a big gush of water came from the faucet above and sent a huge wave through the pipe opening. Ryan and the others were pushed through the rest of the way. Struggling to stay on top, Ryan saw his journal rush by the group and down a long black corridor ahead of them.

"Quick, we've got to catch it! Come on! Swim after it," Ryan shouted.

It was then that he realized they weren't the only water drops. He was surrounded by hundreds of water drops floating in water. He and the Eigenoids were slightly larger and more defined drops, but none the less, there were more drops around them. The drops were talking a weird language and seemed to be having fun swimming about. One accidentally bumped into Ryan.

"Hey, watch where you are going mister. In a hurry," the drop grumbled, pushing Ryan aside.

"Sorry. Just trying to catch up to my friends," Ryan replied, shocked that they could talk.

"You're new," the large drop said.

"Yah. Say, my name is Ryan. What's yours?"

"Name is Drop4356. Ryan, that's a funny name," he laughed.

“Drop4356? What kind of name is that,” Ryan asked.

‘Well, I was drop number 4,356 in my family when I fell from the sky months ago,” the drop replied.

Before he could get into a long conversation with the drop, Newt had swum back to Ryan to bring him up to the group.

“Come on, Ryan. Let’s go get the journal,” Newt shouted, pulling on Ryan’s arm.

“Huh, oh yeah! Almost forgot the journal! Got to go, Mr. Drop4356. Bye,” Ryan yelled as he swam after Newt to catch up.

“Be safe! Stay in the pipe, you young whippersnapper! Stay in the pipe,” Drop4356 shouted at Ryan who didn’t hear him.

Ryan and the Eigenoids were frantically swimming to try and catch up to the journal, which was floating farther and farther away. Surely they would catch up to it sooner or later, before it was too late.

Chapter 10: Burp Drop

Together they hadn't gotten too far when the current started to swirl. Curie had almost grabbed the journal when suddenly she disappeared.

"Hey, where'd she go! Curie, come back," Ryan yelled above the swirling rapids.

"The water is getting faster. It must be a waterfall," Albert shouted.

"Look out, it isn't a waterfall, it is a whirlpool! Hold on," Newt clutched Ryan's arm.

"But, the journal! There it goes! After it," Louis said, diving down to grab the journal. Holding on to each other, they all went down into the center of the whirlpool and disappeared. Ryan felt himself getting squished in his middle. He looked down to only see to his waist. He was stuck!

"Help! I'm stuck! I think I'm stuck in a crack or hole or something," Ryan cried out to anyone who could hear him above the roar of the water. He was kicking his dangling legs as hard as he could.

"Suck it in! I'll pull you through," Albert yelled up to Ryan who was hanging half in a pipe and half out. With a big ker-plunk, Ryan and Albert fell into a bucket of water with a splash.

"Thanks! You got the journal? Where is everybody? You find Curie? She ok," Ryan began rambling so fast that Albert couldn't get a word in edgewise.

"Quiet! Do you mind! I'm trying to grow here," a deep voice commanded.

The Eigenoids all gathered close in a tight huddle. Frightened and shivering, they began to hum as Eigenoids do when they are scared.

"Who - who said that," Ryan said quietly, trying to look around.

He saw a dim light ray peering in where they were huddled. As he turned around, a full 360 degrees, he saw shiny, bumpy metal walls stretching high above them. In fact, he could not see over them. He noticed a massive odd-shaped figure forming next to the group and was so startled he couldn't speak. The mass grew bigger and bigger and soon towered above them. In fear, Ryan shut his eyes and tried to shrink into the huddle. Trembling, he squinted one eye barely enough to sneak a peek at the mass that had grown. The Eigenoids clutched each other tighter.

"I said quiet. I can't think while all that racket is going on," the voice replied. "It's me, Burpy."

Just then, a large pair of eyes seemed to appear and roll from one side of the mass to the other and look straight down on the shivering water drops of Eigenoids and Ryan. Ryan then opened his eyes, as he couldn't stand not knowing what was happening. He saw the eyes look at him and then peer at a couple of other water drops huddled next to them. Suddenly, without warning, they were encased inside of the big mass. They looked as though the mass had simply swallowed them up. They were shouting, but Ryan couldn't hear them. From what he could see, the drops were floating inside of the mass and trying to get out.

Thinking as fast as he could, Ryan tugged on Albert to get the Eigenoids to quiet down. He noticed that it seemed as if the big mass was having problems seeing, and Ryan thought that if they remained quiet, maybe the mass couldn't see them. Albert then noticed the mass as well. He too realized that the mass couldn't see very well, even though he had huge eyes. Together, Ryan and Albert motioned the group to the other side of the room. Slowly, the group swam quietly to the other side to get out of view of the large mass. Ryan then decided to try to communicate with the big mass and find out what was going on. He felt safe out of its sight.

"Burpy? Well, what are you? What do you mean, grow," Ryan asked in a small, calm and quiet voice.

"Don't you know I am the Burp Drop and this is my realm, Water Land. I grow when drops fall into my realm as I eat them and the air they produce. Where are you? I'd like to see and eat, I mean *meet* you. It's ok, you can come out," Burpy replied, rolling his eyes trying to see.

"Eat drops? Why do you eat drops," Albert asked, hiding behind chubby Louis.

"When drops fall, they make a splash and I grow with the air the splash makes," Burpy again replied, trying harder to see.

"Oh, so you are full of air? I see the drops inside of you trying to get out. You mean you are a bubble," Newt spoke as he gained some courage.

"I guess that is what some have called me. Say, enough talk. I can't stay this big for long, I need more drops. Come on over so I can see you. It is rude to stay hidden you know," Burpy said, trying to coax them over to him.

"Nope, nothing doing. We are staying right here until you shrink down to our size. Then we can get acquainted better," Curie said in a scolding manner to the drop.

"So, if this is your realm, where are we? What is this place," Ryan asked.

"How about I give you a riddle. If you guess the riddle, I'll let you go. If not, next wave coming in, I'll find you and then I can greet you my way," the bubble ignored Ryan and boasted as if he was super intelligent.

"Fine by me, give it your best shot," Albert blurted out before anyone could stop him.

"No, it's a trick," Curie said, trying tried to stop Albert, but it was too late.

"Ok, here goes. Two of a kind, not friend, but a pair. One is clean, the other slick. One is thin, the other thick. Beware the later or you will find as beside me you will slide," Burpy then smiled a wide grin and let the drops inside of him swim out.

The Eigenoids huddled together with Ryan and began deliberating on the riddle. Finally after many arguments between Albert and Louis, Newt interrupted their discussion and claimed to know the answer. Trusting him and agreeing with him, they decided to let him give the answer in hopes of being set free.

"Well, Burpy, that was hard, but I think we've got it. We can go free, right," Newt asked for reassurance.

"Fine. If you are right; otherwise, you stay until I need to grow," Burpy said, anxious to hear if they were right.

"Well, the answer is oil and water. Oil and water are always compared together. Oil is slick and thick. Water is clear and thin. Are we right," Newt questioned Burpy.

"Wow, you are correct. Can I still see you? Come on out," Burpy replied.

With much hesitation, the group slowly moved away from the metal walls.

"I did say I'd set you free, but it isn't up to me. I don't control who comes in or who goes out. You will have to wait until I grow big enough and the level is high enough. At that time, something happens and everyone disappears and floats away. It won't be long, now," Burpy replied in sort of a hesitant voice as if he had been caught in a lie and was going to get into trouble.

Ryan was familiar with his tone of voice because he had been caught several times by his Mom for telling a white lie here and there. He noticed the Eigenoids starting to talk quietly among themselves and decided to listen into their conversation. Apparently, Vini had determined that they were in some sort of metal can and that they had fallen through a leak in the pipe. He surmised they had to wait until a human emptied the can so they could escape. The big problem was that no one knew where he or she would be escaping to or where they would end up next.

"Say, Burpy, where does everyone go," Ryan asked.

"Not sure," Burpy replied. "I'm really sorry, guys. Something happens to always dump us out and the drops go their separate ways all over a bumpy brown and green pointy surface."

"Bumpy brown and pointy green surface? A forest? I know. We are going to get dumped onto the ground outside," Ryan exclaimed.

"I think Ryan is right, guys," Albert replied. "Ryan, make sure you have the journal. We are going to need it."

"Maybe I should carry it. I can put inside of my fat belly since you guys seem to loose it often," Louis interjected and stretched for the journal.

"Ryan can carry it in his backpack. He won't loose it again. Will you," Curie asked.

"I can handle it, honest. See," Ryan said as he grabbed the journal away from Louis and placed it in his backpack.

Just then, it got really dark as the water started to swish from side to side within the can. The Eigenoids and Ryan felt themselves being moved. Burpy began to burp and get bigger and bigger as the water splashed waves higher and higher. The Eigenoids and Ryan grabbed hands to hold onto each other so they wouldn't get separated again.

"Here—we—go! Hold on," Newt shouted as loud as he could to overcome the roar of the waves.

Suddenly it was as bright as could be. The can had been moved outside and the sunlight was shining down into the can. It was very bright and warm on the water. It seemed as though they were traveling in the waves forever. In fact, Vini noticed the temperature raising in the water. The sides of the can seemed to be getting hotter the longer they were outside. Without warning, they found themselves riding a huge wave out of the can and splattering onto the ground.

"Ouch! That hurt a bit," cried Ryan.

"Stay together," yelled Albert. "I don't think it is regular ground!"

"Nope, worse. It is sand," Newt replied in a shaky voice.

"What's wrong with sand? It isn't too hard and water soaks into it easy," Curie replied.

"Don't you remember Queen Tiny," Louis reminded her. "Sand is her land. We need to move fast or be captured again."

"At least we are all together. We have the journal this time. And it is light outside. Nothing to fear. We are on track again," Albert stated as he began flipping through the journal and looking around quickly to determine exactly where they landed.

Chapter 11: The Infiltrators

While Albert and Newt began arguing over their exact location, Ryan, Curie, Louis and Vini began to explore their surroundings. It wasn't long before Ryan noticed several sparkling rocks around him. They seemed to glisten brightly in the sun and would appear to move with the light.

"Hey guys! What is the sparkly stuff around me? It is very sharp and pointy like little rocks. I don't recall seeing this in sand. I have a sandbox in my backyard and the sand didn't look like this to me," Ryan said, picking up a couple of rocks.

"Silly, silly boy," Curie replied. "Don't you know what sand is made of?"

"Sure I do," Ryan smirked back quickly in hopes of covering up the fact that he really didn't know the answer.

"Ok. What," Curie promptly replied.

"Well, you know. Sand is, well, it is like dirt but softer and more fine," sputtered Ryan.

"Yes. Close. Good try," Louis interrupted. "You almost got it."

"Sand is made of little grains, or small rocks to us at this size. The sparkly ones are crystals. They typically are like glass. They sparkle because they reflect light. The dull ones are types of rock or other gritty elements. Together they are basically all small pebbles," Curie stated as she picked up a couple of shiny yellow crystals to show Ryan.

"I really like the ones that are shaded purple," Louis interrupted, again.

By now, Newt and Albert even had Vini in their discussion since no one could agree as to exactly where they were. They could tell from the journal that they were ready to begin infiltration, or soaking into the ground. The problem was that they didn't know where they were going to soak. If they soaked into the sand portion of where they fell, it would be easier than the hard edge of the ground. However, soaking into the ground or dirt would be safer because they could try to bypass Sand Land where a tyrant ruler, Queen Tiny ruled.

"Say guys, you got it figured out yet? The ground seems awfully weird. I'm starting to sink. Something is pulling at my feet," Ryan exclaimed and grabbed onto Curie.

"Whatever happens, don't let go until we get there," Newt said as he reached for Ryan's other hand.

"Get where? What's happening," Ryan cried frantically as he clutched tightly onto Newt and Curie.

"Hold on. We're infiltrating," Louis said as he joined hands.

"Wait! Wait! You didn't move from the sand! We shouldn't be on the sand," Albert shouted as he and Vini joined in the circle while Ryan's legs disappeared beneath him.

This happened sooner than Albert or Newt had expected. The ground must have been dry, so when they landed on the sand it quickly began to soak them up. The only thing now was to try to soak quickly past Queen Tiny's tunnels and try to escape without being seen.

"Don't panic, Ryan. You are just soaking into the ground. The loose sand is dry and soaking you up quicker than normal. That's all. When you soak into the sand, look around. It will be hard to see us, so don't let go. We need to stay together. Have fun! It is going to tickle some," Curie told Ryan as she tried to calm him down.

"Yeah, and if you squirm, it will scratch," Louis interrupted again.

"Oh. Ok," Ryan replied, trying to hold still. "Where are we going?"

"I'm afraid we are intruding on Queen Tiny's Sand Land. We will have to be really quiet and fast to get past her," Albert cautioned as Ryan now sank up to his waist.

It didn't take long before Ryan and the Eigenoids were completely submersed into the sand. Ryan seemed to be sinking slower than the rest of the group, so he was getting pulled in two directions from Curie and Newt. As they sank, a sound grew very loud. The earth was shaking so loud that Ryan could hardly hear himself think. The more they sank, the louder the sound grew. The rumble was as loud as a freight train.

"Hey! Slow down," Ryan yelled. "You are going to fast! I can't keep up!"

"I forgot, your pack! It is slowing you down! The pack can't soak as fast as you or the rest of us. You may have to ditch it," Albert shouted back to Ryan.

"No way," Ryan shouted in response. "I'm not leaving it. We need it! I need it! Just slow down a bit so I can keep up."

"We'll try," Newt shouted.

When the Eigenoids finally reached a suitable pace, Ryan tried to look around. The sand was exactly as Curie explained. As they sank, it seemed to get colder and darker. The less light that shined through the crystals, the less colors Ryan could see. Soon, everything had a dark tan color to it and the pretty crystals from the sun had almost disappeared. Ryan did begin to enjoy the sinking. It was starting to tickle his sides as he soaked farther and farther. A couple of times, however, the pack got stuck. As he squirmed to free the pack, he would get scratched from the walls closing in around him. Despite the scratches, he still would not drop the pack that Albert had placed the journal in.

After several delays, the group had reached their intended destination. They found themselves in the middle of an underground tunnel. In fact, it was nothing more than a pathway created by the many ants in the vicinity.

"Well, we're here. Keep quiet. Let's roll or squish for awhile before we sink again. Remember, stay together and keep quiet," Albert tried to caution the group who were giggling loudly from the sinking they had just went through.

"Where is here," asked Ryan. "What is this place? Why is the ceiling so high? Looks like some sort of tunnel or subway."

"You're close again," Louis replied.

"It is an ant tunnel way. We need to keep quiet so we aren't found. Ants hate water you know. They will think we are here to destroy their colony. Keep together and stay quiet," Newt explained.

With a quick double-check of his pack and the journal, Ryan began to squish along and roll forward with the Eigenoids trying very careful to be extra quiet. He had seen ants before, millions of times in fact. He hadn't seen ants that were bigger than him and wasn't anxious to at this point.

While they went forward, Ryan noticed that it was much colder than the surface in the sun. The gritty sand was now smooth and polished on the walls. In fact, the walls seemed to have some kind of coating on them to make them really smooth. Although it was dark and hard to see, every couple of yards there was a glowing substance that acted as hallway lights or nightlights to light their way in the tunnel. Near the glowing bulbs, the walls, floors and ceiling seemed to have glitter sprinkled all over them. It was the crystals in the sand that sparkled like glitter. Ryan had never seen such beauty, nor did he ever imagine it inside of an anthill.

The funniest thing that he saw were bits of old wrappers from bubble gum stuck to the walls like wallpaper. There were bits of food and leaves also ground up and stuck into the walls like pictures. Ryan stopped to look at one wrapper when Albert reminded him to keep moving.

"Would you look at that," Ryan paused for a moment. "Another Double Bubble wrapper. This one has the comic on it."

" Shush! Keep moving," Albert nudged Ryan. "I hear footsteps. We need to hurry before they catch up."

"Sorry. Just never thought my stuff ended up here. Like art," Ryan said and began rolling again.

"Halt," shouted a stern, deep voice.

Just then, Ryan rolled right into a point.

"Hey. That hurt! What's the big idea," Ryan exclaimed.

"Shush, Ryan," Newt scolded Ryan as he grabbed at his arm.

"Quiet! No trespassing in our tunnels. You are under arrest! Let's go," stated a big, tall ant.

Ryan got really quiet and rubbed his eyes. He had never seen such a fierce, large ant before. The ant seemed to tower above him as if it were seven feet tall in the real world. The ant had thick antenna and nimble legs with big bulky arms and chest. It carried a pointy spear made from a stick. Around his waste he wore a belt that had been woven from grass and he had a walnut shell for a helmet. Next to him were three other guards. They too were dressed the same, except they didn't have helmets. Ryan realized that they had no choice but to comply with what they wanted.

"Well, what are your names? Who are you," the big ant began questioning them.

As the ant began looking them up and down, he noticed Ryan's pack on his back. It seemed rather odd for a water drop to have such an item on his back.

Poking at the pack, the guard replied, "What is this thing?"

"That is my backpack," replied Ryan.

By now, the Eigenoids were trying to make a circle to huddle in and hum.

"Stop that, you hear," the main guard said and motioned to his troopers.

"Let's take them to the queen. They are infiltrators! Watch them. They may steal our stuff! Look, this one already stole this thing called a backpack. He must have gotten it from the center room," stated the head guard.

"No I'm not. I'm not a thief. That is my backpack. I carry it with me," Ryan replied in a direct voice.

The Eigenoids were trying to get Ryan to stay quiet, but it wasn't working.

"Well, we'll see about that. Off to the Queen. She is about to host a lunch banquet. We found a picnic going on in the outer world and just got back from the raid. Let's hurry. I want my piece of cake! I heard they that found chocolate, too," the guard said, poking Ryan some more to get him moving.

"As you ordered, sir," shouted the other guards as they all began poking at the Eigenoids and Ryan. The main guard took Ryan's pack and flung it on his back.

"I'll take this, thanks," the big guard stated as he turned to lead them down a tunnel.

The guards lead them down a couple of really steep tunnels. Every once in awhile, they would have to make a sharp turn. Ryan didn't realize how many tunnels and hallways there were inside of an anthill. He began looking around and noticed different corridors that broke into little rooms. Inside the little rooms were big yellow things that looked like soft jellybeans. Smaller ants were patting and talking to the squishy looking pillows. After seeing several of them, Ryan had to ask what they were.

"Mr. Guard, sir. What are those things in the smaller rooms," Ryan asked in a hesitant voice.

"You're kidding, right," replied the guard.

"Well, no. What are they? Are they alive? Why are other ants talking to them," Ryan asked.

"You must be new alright. Those are the Queen's eggs. We are schooling them before they hatch so they can start work right away. You don't need to worry about them. They will hatch long before you get away to steal or destroy them. Let's keep going," the guard said and nudged Ryan along with his spear.

"I don't want to," Ryan started to reply once more, but was interrupted by Albert.

"Oh, don't bother. They don't believe you," Albert replied by kicking one of the spears that was poking at him.

Finally, the walls started to open up and a big opening appeared in front of the group. Ryan was stunned at the huge size of the room he was now standing in. In the center of the room was a large mound with a throne raising up from the middle. Poised very promptly on the throne was an ant that appeared to be very tiny in size. As Ryan and the Eigenoids approached the ant, Ryan noticed a large mass poking through the back of the throne. He now realized that the ant was ten times larger than the huge guard that had brought him to the room. In fact, the gigantic ant on the throne was the Queen.

"Ryan," Albert whispered quietly. "Don't tell the Queen about your journey. She is very picky about outsiders. Don't tell her we are passing through. Just don't say anything."

"He's right, Ryan. Just keep quiet and we'll be ok. We just need your pack back," added Curie.

"Who dares enter my kingdom," the Queen replied as she turned her head around to view the Eigenoids and Ryan.

"Found these infiltrators in sector nine my queen. This odd one was carrying this thing he stole from your center room," the large guard with the helmet stated abruptly as he removed the pack, dropping it onto the ground in front of the Queen.

"Well, a thief among them as well? I should say. What do you have to say, water drops," the Queen commanded them to answer.

Just as Ryan was about to respond, Albert grabbed Ryan's arm and spoke quickly.

"My Queen, we mean you no harm. We were accidentally dumped onto your hill and are looking for a way out. If you would be so kind as to point us to the opening, we will gladly exit your kingdom," Albert replied.

"Accident? I don't think it is an accident that you stole from my center treasure room," the Queen shouted down to the Eigenoids who by now had formed in a circle for protection.

The Queen pointed to her right, to another room. This was the center treasure room. In it, Ryan rubbed his eyes in amazement. Piled high in this room were all sorts of wrappers, food particles and pieces of garbage. He was astounded to think that this was where his garbage ended up and that to the ants, it was some sort of treasure. He saw wrappers from his bubble gum, pieces of fast food French fry containers and even an old shoestring that had broken off from his baseball shoes. In front of the room stood two more armed guards. They looked like the ones in front of the Queen of England's palace. They were straight and tall and did not move a muscle.

Just then, the Queen motioned for the head guard to throw the pack back into the treasure room. With one quick swoop, the pack and the journal were now in a guarded room.

"Time for sentence. I'm tired of you water infiltrators sinking into my realm and destroying my beautiful tunnels, not to mention stealing from us. We work hard you know. We have a picnic to attend. I also have a craving for chocolate cake. Because you stole from me, I will not let you pass. Guards, take them to the outermost corridor of the new extension on the lower level. Seal them into the walls. They can stick there until we are ready to build again and need moisture to form the next tunnel. Since it was so important for them to come down here, let them be here forever in our tunnels! Away with them. Away," Queen Tiny shouted as she threw her hands up in haste.

"Wait," Ryan shouted. "Wait! You can't mean it."

The Eigenoids just held hands and started to hum louder as the guards began poking at them to roll down another corridor.

"Ryan, it will be ok. You'll see," Curie tried to comfort Ryan as they were pushed along.

What had started out to be so pretty and beautiful inside the anthill soon looked dark and scary to Ryan. How could the Eigenoids be so calm? After what seemed like hours of rolling and getting poked, the guards finally came to a halt.

"Well, this is it. We are here. Start sealing, men," the head guard ordered two smaller guards at his side.

One by one, the guards took an Eigenoid and began to dig a hole into the wall. Once the hole was dug, the Eigenoid was forced into the hole and then the ants began spitting on the ground. As they spit on the ground, they formed a door to seal the Eigenoids into the holes. Poor Albert went first. When the ants were done with him, only his little face could be seen in the wall. Ryan began to cry and was very scared. He was trying to pull away from the ants, but the more he pulled, the harder they grabbed at him so he could not escape. The Eigenoids also were scared and began to hum loudly. They tried pulling away, but could not escape the armed guards. Soon, it was Ryan's turn. He began kicking and screaming to let him go, but the ants ignored his pleading. They even laughed at him as they sealed him up.

"Now, quit that noise. You are here and that is all there is to that. Queen Tiny gave the order and there you'll be until we need you for more tunnels. Might as well get comfortable," the head guard said, giving a salute to Ryan and turning away.

"Now what? How will we ever get out? How will I get home? I want my Mommy," Ryan began to cry.

"Ryan, you silly boy. We are water. We can just soak out," Newt replied, trying to calm Ryan down. "Just calm down and concentrate really hard. We can soak our way out."

"What," Ryan asked with a stunned look on his face.

"Watch me! Like we did before," Curie said, soaking out of the wall.

Before she could finish her sentence, she was out and back in the tunnel in front of Ryan.

"Yah, Ryan, come on. Soak it out," Albert said.

Laughing at himself, Ryan said, "Oh. I forgot. Like this?"

Ryan began soaking out of his sealed tomb. One by one the Eigenoids all came together in the tunnel.

"Ok. Let's be really quiet. I think they are almost done with their picnic. They will soon be sleeping off their dinner. This way," Albert said, motioning to the others. He began squishing and rolling back towards the main room where the Queen had been.

"Wait! Not that way. You're headed right for them. Why can't we just soak through around them," Ryan asked as quietly as he could, pulling on Albert's arm to try to stop him.

"No, we have to get your journal. Come on," Albert said persistently.

Quietly they Eigenoids and Ryan all began the journey back through the scary tunnels to the center room. As they approached the room, Ryan began to hear singing and laughing. It was strange, as he never knew that ants had parties. The closer he got to the room, the louder the noise became. Finally, they came to a small corridor they hadn't seen before. It was a side entrance to the treasure room. They were in luck. They could sneak past the guards during the party, grab the journal and backpack and soak their way to the next realm.

"Quickly. In here," Ryan pointed and squished his way through the doorway.

"You found it—the room. Great job, my boy," Newt replied, patting Ryan on the shoulder.

"Hey guys, let's find the pack and get going. If I remember, wasn't there another hazard down here. I just can't put my finger on it. I have a scary feeling about this," Curie said and began looking frantically for the pack.

"I don't know what you're talking about. All I remember is Queen Tiny because she isn't so tiny," Louis replied.

"Yah. You're just chicken, Curie. Quit scaring Ryan. He's been through enough already," Vini said as he too lifted things from around him searching for the pack.

"Hide! Someone's coming," Albert shouted in a half whisper.

Just then, two guards came by and glanced into the room. As they looked from left to right, they didn't see anything outside of the normal garbage, or treasure as they called it. One guard barely missed Ryan's foot as Ryan pulled it quickly under a partial leaf of lettuce he was hiding under. To Ryan's right were Newt and Curie huddling under a bubble gum wrapper. Albert and Vini had climbed inside of a piece of celery that was half eaten and were ducking beneath the edge.

"All looks clear to me," the smaller guard replied.

"Ya, looks fine. Besides those infiltrators were sealed pretty good this time. There was the one funny one, though. You know, the one who cried like a baby for his mommy. What a strange water drop. And that thing he stole. Good thing it is back where it belongs, whatever it was," replied the larger ant.

"Hey, we're missing the big rest. I ate so much cake, my stomach is about to burst. I need to sleep some of this off. Let's go before we don't get a place to lay down. I don't want to get stuck near the opening again. The sun is too bright today," the smaller guard stated as he turned from the treasure room and motioned to his friend.

Ryan happened to peek out from under the lettuce just as they turned away. He had almost been spotted. Luckily he had just missed them.

"Ok. Let's find this pack and get going. All clear, guys," Ryan stated as he kicked off the lettuce.

"That was to close for me, too," Newt stated.

"Found it," shouted Vini. "Hey? What the - Oh no! Quick! Climb the pile! Hurry! Someone help me! It's got me!"

"What? What is it," Ryan spun around to see Vini getting pulled high into the air, dangling by his feet.

While they had been looking for the pack, none of them noticed the plant roots and tree roots growing and slithering in from the corners of the room. They were like snakes looking for rodents; however, they were actually looking for moisture or water to soak up so they could grow. If they managed to soak one of the drops up, there would be no escaping. The Eigenoids quickly scrambled to the top of the pile of garbage and tried to all pull on Vini's arms to free him.

Ryan flung his pack on the pile of garbage. "I think I got something that will work. Hold on, Vini."

Digging through his pack, Ryan pulled out his pair of scissors. He had packed them for an emergency such as this.

"Here. Let me cut you down," Ryan made his way to Vini who was being shaken violently up and down.

"Hurry, up. I'm getting dizzy," Vini replied.

"I got you," Albert and Curie said, grabbing Ryan by the legs as he stretched over the pile to reach Vini.

"Almost. Almost got it," Ryan said. With a loud shriek, he cut the root and Vini fell.

"Thanks! That'll teach it. Crazy root," Vini kicked garbage at the hurt root as it shrank back into the wall.

"Better show some respect, Vini. It might come back," Albert warned.

"Here they come again," Curie cried. "I told you I remembered something else was here."

"Take my hand, Vini. Quick," Ryan shouted and he pulled Vini to the top of the pile.

"Now, what do we do? How do we get past those things? They will start climbing this pile soon."

"I know, the journal. What does it say? Doesn't it have a map," Albert asked.

"Take a look. Quick," Ryan said as he pulled the journal out and passed it to Newt.

"Let's see. Here we are. Yes, there it is. The crack. It should be right over there," Newt pointed between two celery sticks.

To the left of the pile were two celery sticks that had been positioned like pillars. Between them was a small crevice. With all the commotion, no one had noticed it before.

"So, how do we get there past the roots," Ryan said, pointing to two roots closing in on the crack.

"That's not to difficult. Grab those pieces of gum wrapper over there," Vini said, pointing next to Louis who was getting ready to bite into a piece of brownish apple core.

The Eigenoids all looked at Louis like he was crazy. How could he really be thinking of food at a time like this? How could he be thinking of eating something so gross as a browning apple core?

"What? What are you looking at? So I'm a bit nervous and scared and try to eat when I can? It is nourishing you know. Apples are good for you," Louis replied, looking puzzled at them and acting as if he wasn't doing anything wrong.

"Ok. I won't ask how you plan to eat when you are water. But, hand me the foil wrappers next to you and put the apple core down," Vini responded quickly.

"Guys! Hurry up, will you. The roots are getting pretty close to start climbing and I don't want to get sucked up. Do you," Curie warned again.

"Let's get in a line and hide under the foil. We can walk to the crevice. The roots will get their reflection in the foil and not notice us under it. We can slip right by them," Vini stated as he started motioning for them to form a line.

"Awesome! I'll lead," Albert said, jumping to the front of the line.

One by one they got into a line. Louis had to hustle to pick up the rear as the gang started down the hill towards the crevice. A couple of times, one or two of them slipped and knocked garbage down the pile.

"Be careful. We can't let the roots think we are under here," Newt scolded and helped Louis up as he again slipped.

As they approached the tip of one root, which was searching eagerly, they had to stop and sink low so their feet did not show. After a brief pause in movement, the root turned and went another direction. Breathing a sigh of relief, they continued on towards the crevice. At the crevice, Albert looked into the crack and tried to assess the situation.

"Looks endless. I can't see any light or bottom. It has to be it. It just has to," Albert mumbled.

"Endless? No bottom? Is that what you said," Ryan choked on his words and took a big gulp.

"Albert, is it dark," Newt asked.

"Yep. I'm sure it is it. Let's go," Albert stepped aside and motioned his arm for Ryan to go first.

"What? Me? How do I," Ryan said, backing up and stumbling into the Eigenoids behind him.

"Oh, come now. Trust me, my boy," Albert said, trying to reassure him.

"Hurry up! They're coming. I think they figured us out," Curie yelled as she pushed the Eigenoids forward again.

Louis started to roll forward to escape a root. Newt pushed Ryan and Curie pushed Newt.

"Just jump already, Ryan," Newt said with a loud voice.

"Just go," the Eigenoids shouted in unison.

"Ok. Ok. I'm going. Here goes nothing," Ryan's voice faded as he jumped into the crevice and began falling down and down.

Chapter 12: Rock Land

Following right behind Ryan came Newt, Albert, Curie and lastly, Louis. Ryan had his pack with the journal and his supplies clutched tightly in his hands. A couple of times he seemed to get stuck as the walls began to narrow. Once there was even a backup that he caused from getting tangled on the pack straps. Finally, they started to feel slippery against the walls. It was getting ticklish again and Ryan wasn't so scared. He remembered that funny feeling and was sure things would be fine.

Suddenly, one by one they plopped out of a crevice in a ceiling and fell onto a large boulder.

"Ouch," yelped a large voice. "Stop that."

"Sorry, sir. I was in a hurry to escape the roots," Albert replied cautiously.

"Say, your voice sounds familiar. You wouldn't happen to be Rocker, would you," Newt said with a loud happy voice.

"Why, yes. Yes I am! Who's asking? I can't see you," replied the large boulder that the Eigenoids and Ryan had fallen onto.

"Oh, sure. Come on guys. It's Rocker," Newt interjected and began to slide to the base of the rock.

Together the Eigenoids all followed Newt to the base of the boulder. Rocker was a large boulder made of shale and other elements in the ground. He was Newt's oldest friend from the water cycle. Rocker had been around for centuries and traveled many miles beneath the surface. As the Earth's plates moved, he would slowly move as well. Newt never really knew when they would meet. It usually was an accident such as this. Rocker was also the largest occupant in Rock Land. Rock land was the land that was found beneath Sand Land and above Coal City. The Eigenoids knew they would be safe here for a while. They couldn't wait to visit with their old friend.

"It is us, the Eigenoids. Remember us? It has been quite a while since we last came to visit," Newt responded joyfully.

"Eigenoids! Boy, I haven't seen you since I was a pebble," Rocker grumbled as he tried to smile.

"Oh, come now, you - a pebble? That's like calling me skinny, like Newt," Louis replied.

"Same old Louis. How the heck are you guys? Say, who's the new fella with you? You look kind of different don't you for an Eigenoid," Rocker said as he stared at Ryan.

"Oh, him. Allow me to introduce, Ryan. He's our new keeper. Remember, George. Well, Ryan is his grandson. George grew too old. Ryan now takes care of us," Albert explained.

"Say, Hi, Ryan," Curie said, nudging Ryan forward.

"Uh - Hello," Ryan said.

Ryan was amazed that a rock could talk and had regular features like a face. He had never noticed a face on a rock before, but this rock seemed to have a full face that appeared and disappeared, as it would speak. Ryan also noticed that the longer he looked at the rock, the easier it was to see his surroundings. As before, his eyes had to focus. He decided to open his pack and pull out his flashlight so he could see well.

"No," shouted Vini. "Don't turn it on! The light will blind the rocks and reflect something awful."

"Oh, sorry. Didn't mean to," Ryan said, stopping just in the nick of time.

"That's ok, my boy. You'll learn," Rocker replied. "So, you are the new guy to take care of my friends, huh? First time coming down here?"

Rocker's face would appear and form as he spoke and began to question Ryan.

"I guess so. Yes. I haven't been here before," Ryan said, putting the light back in his pack.

"Hey, Newt. Have a new one myself. Say hello to Junior," Rocker rolled his eyes to his right where a smaller rock was rolling towards them.

"Hello! I'm Junior. Pleased to meet you," spouted a small voice.

"Well, hello," the Eigenoids responded together.

Ryan spun around to look at the smaller rock. It was a pale green color and had small, jagged edges on one side. Yet, despite the edges, the rock was still able to roll in a wobbly fashion. Ryan noticed the face appear and disappear on the rock as it spoke just like the boulder. When the face appeared, it had a small nose and eyes as well, and a funny little mouth that curled up on one side.

"Ahhh," the little rock yawned and blinked his eyes.

"Tired, my son," asked Rocker.

"Yep. Rolling takes a lot out of you," Junior replied.

"That's contagious. I'm actually sort of tired myself. Escaping ants and roots will wear you out, too," Curie replied with a yawn.

"Say, not to be rude, but can we rest here before we move on? I know it is safe from roots," Albert asked Rocker.

"I guess so. I've missed our visits. Stay as long as you want. You can rest on me if you want, or over on the shelf to the right. I was hoping you'd stay awhile," Rocker said with a happy tone.

"Daddy, tell me a story. You always do before I sleep. Please," Junior begged as he yawned again.

"Well, ok. I know just the thing. Newt, you tell the story about how we met. I bet Ryan would like that one. Wouldn't you boy," Rocker said, coaxing Newt who loved to tell tales.

One by one the Eigenoids rolled and squished over to the shelf or ledge that was to the right of Rocker. Ryan decided to use his pack as a pillow and rest his head while he listened to Newt tell his story. As Ryan made himself comfortable, he noticed several other water drops join them. Before long, water drops surrounded them. As Ryan sat up, he rubbed his eyes in disbelief. The water drops were changing into funny dust particles. Everything began to glow and suddenly the water drops were all Eigenoids.

"Ryan! Ryan! Here are some of our cousins! Come meet them," Albert shouted.

"Hi! Hello! How are you? Awful big ain't he," replied a slur of voices from the many Eigenoids surrounding Ryan.

"Pleased to meet you," Ryan replied.

Albert went on to explain and introduce each one of the new guests. Some were short and some were tall. Some had weird hair like Albert. Most had hair like Newt. Strangely, each had it's own shade or color to them from light green to dark blue. Ryan was tired, and although he too wanted to visit and talk to get to know them, he was really tired and could hardly keep his eyes open.

"Ok. Ok. Settle down, guys. I need to tell my story. You want to hear it, don't you," Newt said as he waved his arms up and down to settle the crowd that had amassed.

"Shhhh," Curie added with a soft voice. "Go for it, Newt. We're all ears."

"Well, it all started years ago. Rocker was a bit smaller than he is now. I, myself was younger and didn't need my spyglass," Newt started to speak.

"Come now, Newt. You were skinnier, too," Louis interrupted.

"Yes. And skinnier. Anyway, to continue, I was younger and having fun with the roots. You see, roots is roots. They think they are so special, but we all know that they can think that as long as we know better. I used to test my theories about speed and momentum by getting roots to chase me. I was fast and they could never catch me. Mom always warned me, but I never listened. Who does, right," Newt said, continuing his story.

"Newt," Curie said, scolding her friend.

Rocker had to laugh along with the rest of the Eigenoids because they all agreed with him.

"Ok. So, I was teasing the roots and fading in and out between a water drop like I am now, and my regular form. As a drop, I moved a bit slower, and as myself, well, super speedy. At one point, I tripped and a root almost caught me. I quickly transformed into my regular self and fell through a crevice. You know, like the one we took to get here."

Ryan was really interested in Newt's story so he propped himself up from his backpack. As he continued to listen, Newt's voice seemed to become a monotone sound or noise and he soon fell fast asleep. The Eigenoids knew he needed his rest and let him sleep. They on the other hand, urged Newt to continue since his story was getting exciting.

"Look, Ryan's asleep," Curie said, interrupting Newt. "Try to keep it down. The boy needs his rest."

Newt began to make himself a bit more comfortable as he continued. "Just as we did today, I fell right on top of Rocker."

"Yep. Sure did. You were cold and wet and slimy feeling, too. You really tickled," Rocker said, laughing to himself.

"Well, I sure didn't expect you beneath me, but you broke my fall. That was great! Anyway, I fell right on top of Rocker, like I said. No sooner did I roll off of him when a root, which had followed me through the crevice, snatched me! It was mad. Mad I tell you."

"Say, I thought roots couldn't go through rock," Albert and Vini tried to correct Newt.

"I didn't say they went through rock. I said they chased me through the crevice. Listen and pay attention. They chased me through the crevice since they were so mad and apparently, thirsty. In fear of my life, I started to run as fast as I could, but I was trapped. Rocker, who I woke up from his nap, saw that I was trapped. He felt sorry for me and without thinking, he rolled right in front of the crevice. As he did—SCREECH," Newt yelled.

"What happened? Did he roll over you," a smaller Eigenoid asked.

"Now, how could he have done that? I'm here ain't I," Newt said laughing loudly and patting the head of the small Eigenoid who was quite embarrassed by his loud guess. "You see, the screech was the root. When he rolled to cover the crevice, he accidentally cut the root off. He saved my life. We've been best friends ever since. The End."

"Yep. Best buds," Rocker added. "Good story, Newt. Boy, I've missed you. Look, Junior is asleep, too. Awesome job. Awesome."

"Tell another. Please," the littlest Eigenoid cried out.

Newt began again with another story; but another Eigenoid by the name of Alf had to interrupt Newt. Alf was one of the oldest Eigenoids from the Inner Realm. He was treated like an elder and when he spoke, everyone listened to him. He usually reserved his words for emergencies or information of grave importance. If he spoke, they listened.

"Newt, my son. It is good to see you and your other friends. I'm glad to see you are doing well and have found allies in both realms," Alf spoke with a raspy voice.

Newt replied with respectful gestures, "Why, thank you, sir. We're also glad to see some of our dearest cousins and friends as well. How are things down here?"

Newt stopped his story with the interruption and waited to hear the elder speak. Curie and Albert both perked up and nudged Louis who had started to snore quite loudly.

"I must warn you, now that you've had your fun and we've had a chance to visit, it still isn't safe in the Inner Realm. The king who banished you, King Odious, is still on the rampage after all this time. He threatens to banish anyone who helps or gives you refuge. You see, he has heard about your legendary trips through whispers and is furious. I came to give you warning," Alf spoke with caution.

"Banish," Rocker interrupted the conversation. "Not me! I'm sorry, guys. Missing you or not, you'll have to go. Can't be banished, not me. I've got Junior now, you know."

"Wow, didn't even think those trips would get out. No problem old friend. We'll get moving on. Ryan did get a bit of rest. We know we just got here, but don't want any trouble for you," Albert said.

"I'll miss you," Newt replied.

"Ryan, wake up boy. Come on. Time to go," Albert nudged Ryan who was fast asleep.

"Go? We just got here. I'm tired. Let me rest just a bit more. Please," Ryan yawned and rolled back over to face the wall.

"Nope. Got to go. Bye cuz," Curie said, giving the last Eigenoid a hug as they slowly turned back into water drops and started rolling away.

"Ryan, let's go," Newt grabbed the pack beneath Ryan's head.

"Junior, can you roll a bit to your left? I think there is another crevice over there," Rocker said in a commanding voice to get Junior's attention.

"Oh, like this," Junior rolled to the right.

"No, your other left. You know the one you never get," Rocker laughed.

"Oops. Here. Got it," Junior said, laughing as he rolled left.

"This should take you to Coal City. Say Hi to Jimmy Black for me," Rocker said bidding them good bye.

"Thanks old friend. I'll never forget you. Hopefully we'll meet again," Newt began to get really squishy and sad as he rolled towards the crevice.

One by one they were off again. As they came to the crevice, Curie jumped in to follow Newt. Next came Louis and then Ryan. Vini jumped and Albert was last. They fell down and down into pitch black darkness.

Chapter 13: Blackness

Blackness was all around the Eigenoids and Ryan as they dropped through the crevice. In fact, it was so dark that Ryan couldn't see his hand in front of his face. He had to feel his way around in order to locate the Eigenoids who were also blinded by the blackness. In addition to the blackness, it became extremely cold and clammy. Ryan and the Eigenoids soon began to panic. As usual, the Eigenoids all grabbed hands and began to hum. In doing so, they started to emit the funny glow they made before. This glow was enough to enable Ryan to grab his pack, which he had dropped. Quickly he pulled out his flashlight so they could see.

"What is this place? I don't like it here," Ryan said.

Suddenly a congested voice began coughing. "Well, welcome. You are in Coal City. Passage to the Caverns and world to Jimmy Black, diamond in the rough."

"Uh - hello," Ryan responded trying to be as polite as possible.

"Jimmy! Rocker says Hi. It's us - Newt, Albert and the gang. Meet our friend, Ryan. He's new. We're here for visits and such," Newt stated in his happy voice.

"Boy am I glad to see you guys. The Eigenoids don't come by here anymore," Jimmy replied.

"I know it has been awhile. You heard what happened, that we got banished, right? Last time we came as a surprise, you weren't here. We missed you. That was years ago, though. How've you been," Newt replied.

"Well, could be better. Will be now that you are here," Jimmy muttered in a sad voice.

"Why so glum? You say we don't come by anymore? Why did everyone leave you? We used to like to get dirty every once in awhile," Louis questioned Jimmy.

Jimmy explained what happened while they were gone. He had been hoping to find Eigenoids to turn him into a diamond. Jimmy had a younger brother that had crossed paths with King Odious. King Odious had gotten extra dirty and Jimmy's brother, Sprat, offended King Odious and his throne by rubbing in the extra dirt. It was all in fun, or so his brother thought. As his punishment, King Odious turned Sprat into a diamond by squeezing him too tight with heat and pressure. When humans came by and found him, they took Jimmy's brother away. Jimmy had not seen him in years.

"That's terrible, Jimmy," Curie said, beginning to cry for him.

"Yes. Just terrible," Vini agreed.

"So, can you help me turn into a diamond so I can find my brother," Jimmy asked.

"I'm afraid not. We don't have as much strength as King Odious to generate that much heat," Albert stated as he tried to do some calculations in Ryan's journal. "Nope, not enough."

"Excuse me, Jimmy. I'm not really sure you would want to be a diamond. We, I mean humans, take diamonds and break them down into rings and such for jewelry. I'm afraid you may never see your brother again," Ryan said, turning to face Jimmy, the large black rock next to him.

"He doesn't mean break apart. Not your brother. He may have been kept as one big diamond, right Ryan," Curie nudged Ryan to quickly change his statement before Jimmy got upset.

"Oh, that's right. He probably was kept in one piece. In fact, they probably cleaned him up bright and shiny and put him in a store window. I'm sure that is what happened," Ryan quickly understood Curie and changed his story.

"You think so? Really," Jimmy asked for reassurance.

Trying to be calming, Vini agreed and Jimmy was satisfied. He believed his brother was safe.

"I guess he'll be ok, if you say so, boy," Jimmy replied. "I just hope that Odious comes back so I can take care of him. I owe him one for sure."

"Well, you may get your chance if we don't get going soon. I heard there is still a bounty on us and anyone who helps us," Newt cautioned Jimmy.

"Guys, I feel itchy and weird," Ryan began to comment in a funny voice.

"Oh, you are getting dirty. No biggy. We can't stay long anyway. If we get too dirty as water, we turn to mud and then we can't go on in the cycle. I guess we better not stay here too long," Albert warned.

"Albert's right, Jimmy. We can't stay this time. We'll be back as Eigenoids though, soon. When we return again, we can help get your brother or at least take care of Odious sometime," Vini responded with a fierce gesture of an imaginary sword fight.

"I understand. Glad to know you are still around and able to help. My crevice is just to the right a bit. It is quite the aquifer now. Have fun," Jimmy smiled with a big gray grin and said good bye.

"Thanks Jimmy. See you 'round," Newt replied as he followed Curie and Louis to the crevice.

"See ya," Albert waved and tugged at Ryan to follow them as they left.

As they made their way to the crevice, Ryan had many questions about Jimmy and getting dirty. Albert explained that as the water drops absorb their surroundings, the particles of dust from the coal stick to them and sink inside them. This turns them into thick muddy drops that won't allow them to pass through to the underground Cavern. In addition, if they stayed long enough they would possibly harden as the moisture would get pushed out and could turn into little pieces of coal dirt. The rule was that they never stayed in Coal City as water. They could visit as often as they wanted as regular form, just not as water.

Ryan placed his flashlight back in his pack and grabbed Albert's hand. Together they jumped into the crevice to join the others in the large aquifer.

Chapter 14: The Brother's Twins

Plop! Plop! One by one the Eigenoids fell beneath Ryan into a puddle of water.

"Aren't you coming, Ryan," Curie shouted up to Ryan who was dangling from the crevice.

"I'm trying. I hate dangling like this. It is really getting old. Can't you guys help me," Ryan shouted down to the Eigenoids who were swimming about and splashing at each other.

"Can't you are too high to reach," Albert yelled.

"Suck it in, remember," Louis shouted with a laugh.

"Ok. Here I go. Get ready," Ryan said as he sucked in his stomach with all his might.

Nothing happened. All of a sudden, he did start to slide, not drop. He noticed that he was sliding down what appeared to be a big spiked rock hanging from the ceiling of the huge cave.

"Hee, hee, hee. That tickles, matey. A bit lower. There you go, right there. Ahhh," a quirky, shrill voice giggled.

"Huh? Who said that," Ryan asked .

"I did," the voice replied.

"Quit that! It's my turn," replied another voice that was just as silly sounding, but at a lower pitch.

"Guys. I don't think we're alone down here," Ryan slowly said.

"Seriously, that tickles! I love it. Keep it up. You can go to the other side if you want," the high-pitched, silly voice repeated again.

"When's my turn? Don't you want to tickle me," the lower voice sounded.

"Who are you," Ryan asked.

"Don't you mean what are we," the small voice giggled.

"No. He means, what are we not," the low voice spoke in a chuckling fashion.

"No, I mean WHO are YOU," Ryan repeated his question.

"Ok. Don't get stretched out of shape. Get it—stretched," the small voice could hardly get his words out as he laughed loudly.

"Good one! Good one! How about, don't get dropsy! Get it? Dropsy," the lower voice laughed and made all kinds of waves in the stream where the Eigenoids were floating.

"No way. Not you guys! What luck? Now what do we do," Newt asked, looking up to see Ryan still hanging by the straps of his pack and staring into a pair of silly looking eyes.

"It can't be. Are you sure, Newt," Albert asked.

"Ryan, pull hard on your bag to free the bag from the rock. You can drop that way. Hurry before he sticks you to tight," Vini yelled up to Ryan. "We're not in an aquifer, we're in the Caverns!"

Ryan braced his feet against the rock and began pulling with all of his might. Slowly he started to drop. Without warning, he freed himself and dropped quickly into the stream below. Once in the stream he could look up and see what he had been stuck on and who had been talking to him. The funny giggles were coming from a long, spiked rock hanging from the ceiling. It had lots of colors on it and a funny face that faded in and out. Each time it laughed, different funny expressions appeared. After watching the faces, Ryan soon realized that the same face never appeared twice. He had counted up to ten faces when he finally asked what the creature was.

"What is that," Ryan asked Albert who swimming next to him.

Albert, grabbing Ryan's pack replied, "That is Stan up there."

"And, over here is Stag," the deep voice interjected with a laugh.

"What's so funny? Your names," Ryan asked.

"Our names? He thinks our names are funny," Stag responded back with a question to Stan.

"No? He thinks your name is Funny. Mine is Stan," Stan responded in a laughing manner again.

"Didn't your mother ever teach you manners," Curie said, scolding them for laughing.

"Manners? Nope. Can't say she taught him. Never met either. Did you, Stag," Stan joked.

"Nope, never met Either. I bet Either and Manners were brothers. Were they," Stag continued.

"Ryan, I need the map. Just ignore them. They are crazy twins. They are very funny, but dangerous. We need the map to find the right path out of here. Help me, will ya," Albert said quietly.

"Oh. Ok. Here you go," Ryan whispered as he pulled the map from the pack and handed it to Albert.

"While Albert looks at the map, I'll tell you about the twins," Newt said, approaching Ryan to help guard him from getting too close to Stag. "They are crazy twin spires of rock. Stan is the one in the ceiling. He is a stalactite. Stag is the spire sticking up from the ground through the water and is a stalagmite. They compliment each other all the time and use jokes to catch water drops off guard. They will try anything to get you laughing so that you forget to try to leave because you are having so much fun. Before you know it, you are stuck to them like glue and can't escape. As water drips on them it spreads minerals onto them. This helps them grow, but it also tickles them something fierce. To listen to them for too long can be deadly. They are fun at first; but be careful they don't pull you into their world of jokes and nonsense. Best to stay by us."

"Problem, everyone. The map shows two tunnels but it didn't mark the one we took," Albert motioned the group together.

Just then, Stag spoke up to interrupt, "Two you say you see, but friend or foe, I see three - hee, hee, hee."

The Eigenoids and Ryan looked over the map and saw three tunnels. The map marked two. Now they were all confused. Looking closer, Vini noticed a note at the bottom of the map. It read:

"Trick them for the truth by getting one to tell a lie."

Each Eigenoid tried to come up with something to trick them into telling a lie that they would try to pass off as the truth. Then they would know which one to go through to escape. Unfortunately, none of them could think of anything that would help. Ryan began to ponder as well. It was getting increasingly harder to concentrate with all of the talk and giggling going on between the twins. Finally, Ryan solved the riddle and began to ask a question.

"I have two, you have three, if a foe I be, which is not for me," Ryan asked Stag.

"What? Let me think," Stag responded seriously, for the very first time.

"You did it, my boy," Vini replied.

"How? I don't get it," Albert said nudging Newt.

"Shhhh. I'll explain. We have two tunnels in the map. They have three tunnels ahead, right," Newt explained.

"I got that far. Keep going," Albert insisted.

"Well," Newt said, "it is like an experiment in logic. If we were foes, we wouldn't want to stay, right? We would want to leave. If we want to go, then he is asking for them to tell him the tunnel that he would not want. Meaning he wants the tunnel that would keep him here. Knowing they would lie, they will tell him the tunnel that actually leads to the way out."

"Well, I'm waiting," Ryan said impatiently.

"We need a bit more time," Stan replied.

"I know. You don't want the middle one! Nope, definitely not the middle," Stag quickly sounded.

"Thanks! Ok, let's go guys. The middle it is. That wasn't too hard," Ryan gloated with pride.

"What? He said NOT the middle," Stan chirped back and then started laughing.

"Yah. Not the middle, I said," replied Stag.

"But you guys are so backwards I figured you may not tell the truth so that means the middle is what I really want if I am a foe," Ryan responded.

"Say, how'd you figure that out so quickly little one," Stag questioned him.

"I play games like this with my Pa-Pa and Dad a lot. They can never beat me," Ryan said with a smile as he and the Eigenoids began to swim away to the middle tunnel.

"It was sure lots of fun. Be safe! Happy trails," Stag replied as the Eigenoids and Ryan traveled farther and farther and farther away.

"Trails? Don't you mean pails? Get it Pails," Stan replied laughing and giggling.

The twins began again with their heckling back and forth and laughter filled the echoes of the tunnel as Ryan and the Eigenoids made their way to the outside world. In the distance, Ryan saw a bright light. Curiosity filled Ryan as they traveled closer. The cavern opened up wide and the rainbow of colors soon surrounded Ryan.

"Say, guys. That Stag was a pretty nice, funny character after all," Ryan told the group.

"Yah. Of the two, he is the nicer one. Stan seems to get really annoying at times, though," Curie responded.

"Finally, we're here," Albert shouted for joy.

Chapter 15: Monsters Abound

The Eigenoids cheered at reaching the opening of the cavern. Lying before them was warm sunshine and the passage to nature. Eigenoids truly loved the outdoors because most of their work was displayed in the Animal Kingdom's natural state. Ryan rubbed his eyes as he floated into the warm sunshine. The world looked, smelled, tasted and sounded much different than he had ever sensed it before. It was truly something to behold.

As Ryan and the Eigenoids floated calmly into the light, Newt and Albert began to take turns resting their heads on Ryan's pack. They all joined hands to form a circle and float as they decided to rest a while.

"Say, Curie, I never noticed it before, but things seem to almost glisten in the sunshine. Is that the way it always looks from this size," Ryan asked.

"Not always. Typically only after a rain shower," Curie replied.

"Oh," Ryan said as he looked around.

"Who said rain," Newt claimed as he raised his head quickly, upsetting the pack and everyone on it.

"I said it only glistens this way after a rain. Pay attention, Newt," Curie scolded.

"Quick, look for the rainbow," Albert shouted to the group.

The Eigenoids quickly raised their heads and began looking all around in the sky for a rainbow.

"And why is a rainbow so important, may I ask," Ryan asked Albert.

"Rats! We've missed it. I bet one is coming though. Looks like a bit more rain, too," Louis said with a look of disappointment.

"We can use the rainbow to travel to Puffy the Cloud. As the sun heats up the Earth, the water will turn into vapor and we'll evaporate to the cloud," Albert explained to Ryan.

"Oh. Well, I guess we will have to wait to catch a rainbow, then," Ryan said, leaning his head back to take in the surroundings.

"Guys, doesn't it smell sort of weird? I really smell something funny," Louis said, wrinkling his nose as best as he could.

"Yah. I smell something awful! Smells like rotten eggs," Ryan said, grabbing at his nose with his stubby arms.

"Look out Ryan! You're headed for a snare," Curie cried, trying to reach out for Ryan.

"What is that thing," Ryan asked with amazement.

"It is a cage to catch small freshwater animals like crayfish," Albert warned.

"But what smells," Ryan asked.

"Look to your right. See the terrible garbage and waste from the humans. It is littered all along the shoreline. It is rotting garbage. It has gotten really bad compared to what it used to be. You know, cans, food wrappers, fishing lures, dead bait—you name it, it is there," Albert said.

"Uh, guys. I think it is moving. Better swim faster! Hurry it up. Something is coming," Newt shouted.

"Help! Something has grabbed my pack! Help," Ryan shouted at the top of his voice.

Just as Ryan had turned to swim, a piece of fishing string that had been left on the shore tangled around the pack. It was pulling Ryan and the pack closer to the shore and to the garbage. Suddenly a groaning sound could be heard coming from the garbage wrapper on the shore. As Ryan was fighting the line for his pack, he began to notice fuzzy greenish gray stuff on the garbage wrapper that had been left on the shore. Just then, as if the line pulling at him wasn't enough, a bird swooped down and snipped at the line. The line broke and sent Ryan and the pack hurling back into the deeper water away from the bank.

"There you go fella," tweeted a small pipe-like sound.

"Oh thank you," said Ryan, clutching his pack tightly.

"Yes, thanks," shouted the Eigenoids.

"That was a close one, my boy," Albert said as he patted Ryan on the back.

"Um—Hello," Ryan said as he composed himself. "Who, are you?"

"Tweet. I am Sam. Sam Sparrow at your service," the small, frail bird tweeted in response.

"Sam, what's with all the garbage," Albert asked.

"Don't know. Humans seem to dump stuff over that hill up there and it rolls down here to the water," Sam said, fluttering his wings.

Just then another moan came from the garbage. A gust of moldy smell came like steam from the pile. The Eigenoids, the sparrow and Ryan all looked in fear at the pile on the shore.

"Quick. Hide," the Sparrow shouted as he started to fly away. "The monster will get you if you get too close!"

The Eigenoids swam behind a tin can and peered over the edge at the pile, which seemed to be moving up and down like it was breathing. Again, moans and now snorts came from the pile.

"Who's over there," Ryan shouted from behind the can.

"What? Keep it down. I'm trying to take a nap. Can't you let a guy get any rest around here," a voice replied.

"Uh, sorry. Who are you? What are you," Newt said, tugging at Ryan who was standing up by now.

"Me? I'm Bouregard the Beaver. You can call me Bo for short," said the baby beaver as he poked his head out from under the garbage wrapper on the shore.

"A beaver," Ryan laughed. "We thought you were a monster trying to eat me."

"Hi, we're Eigenoids and this is Ryan," Albert said as he stood up trying to be brave.

"Well, hello," Bouregard replied.

"Didn't mean to disturb you," Curie replied, swimming a bit closer. "Say, what's this hooked to your tail and around your feet?"

"I'm not sure. It really hurts! I found it yesterday and can't get it off," Bouregard replied starting to cry and tug at the fishing line.

"I thought you were pulling me in by trapping me with the line. I pulled back and that must have made it tighten more. I'm sorry," Ryan said as he swam closer.

"Quick, Ryan. In your pack. Still have the scissors," Vini asked Ryan, pointing to his backpack.

"Great idea! I can cut him loose! Hold still, this won't hurt a bit," Ryan said as he opened his pack.

Ryan reached into his pack and took out the scissors to cut the beaver loose.

While cutting the line, which had become tangled around Bouregard's feet and tail, Ryan began to ask questions.

"How's come you couldn't cut the line with your beaver teeth," Ryan asked as he snipped loose Bouregard's tail.

"Well, I tried, but every time I took a swipe at it, it got stuck between my two front teeth and I couldn't get it loose enough to grab it with my paws. Thanks so much," Bouregard said with joy as he could see that his tail was free.

"How'd you get all tangled in this mess in the first place," Newt asked as he helped Ryan cut loose his back left paw.

"Don't really know. I was making my way to a small bendy tree over to the right a ways when my feet got stuck on some paper stuff. Next thing I knew, I had this thing - line you call it, - twisted around one foot. The more I tried to get loose, the more this monster tangled me up. I drug it with me all day and all night. It was picking more and more stuff up," Bouregard said as he stretched his left paw that had now been cut free.

"How's that feel," Ryan said as he reached for the other paw.

"Well, pretty good," Bouregard said, stretching some more.

"Last one. Hold still," Ryan said. He had to squish a bit onto Bouregard's fur to get a good grip on the line.

"That tickles," Bouregard said with a giggle.

"Wait for it. There," Ryan said, snipping the last line.

"Thank you," Bouregard cried as he was free. "That monster won't get me no more!"

Just then the sparrow returned. He looked down at the Eigenoids and the funny beaver all laughing and talking.

"Where's the monster? Did he chase you? Did you chase him? Where'd he go," the sparrow asked, tweeting loudly.

"Sam, meet your monster. This is Bouregard - I mean, Bo. He's a beaver, not a monster," Curie said as she introduced Bouregard.

"A beaver? Where's my monster? I can see he's a beaver," Sam now squawked in anger.

"No. Your beaver was the monster. You didn't see he was a beaver because of all of the garbage tied up on him from the line," Curie replied.

"Oh. Well, then. Hi Bo. I'm Sam," Sam replied as he started to swoop down to try to grab some of the wrappers for a nest.

"I wasn't the monster. The stuff called line was. It grabbed me and tangled me up so I couldn't get away. In fact, it was grabbing more stuff every time I tried to move. Every time I moved, something else got stuck to me," Bouregard cried. "I am so happy you came. If I can ever help you, let me know."

"Well, it is starting to sprinkle in the distance. Can you take us to the rainbow before it goes away," Albert asked.

"Sure! Hop on. Us beavers are fast swimmers you know. Just grab a piece of hair and hang on. My hair is water-resistant so it is hard for water to stay on. I usually don't give rides so you have to hold on tight! Here we go," Bouregard said as he leaned over to the Eigenoids.

One by one the Eigenoids and Ryan jumped onto Bouregard's hair for a ride. Bouregard swam as fast as he could and made it to the rainbow with minutes to spare.

"Thanks Bo. Sorry about all the garbage that hurt you, Ryan said as he patted the hair he had been holding. "When I get back I'll let people know how bad they hurt animals in the Animal World by their garbage. I'll never hurt you guys again. I promise," Ryan said as he crossed his hand where his heart would be.

"I thought you looked funny for an Eigenoid water drop. So you are human," Bouregard asked.

"Yes. I am a boy. The Eigenoids are my friends and are taking me on a water trip through the water cycle," Ryan replied.

"Well, how much farther have you got to go," Sam asked. "Where did you start?"

"Well, don't know exactly," Ryan replied.

"He started at the beginning, you crazy bird," Bouregard said, looking up at the sparrow that was mumbling with garbage wrappers stuffed in his mouth.

"Not exactly. You see, we can't find the beginning. We've been looking for the start ever since we came and we can't find it. You know, the start of the water cycle. The beginning of the aqua," Albert said.

"Um - Albert. Albert. There is no beginning," Louis replied softly.

"What do you mean, no beginning? Sure there is," Albert responded.

"Uh - he's right, Albert," Ryan replied. "We can't be looking for the start of the water cycle. It is a cycle."

Chapter 16: Reunion

While they traveled up into the sky, Ryan saw many things below from a different light. He began to turn into vapor as he evaporated. He became very thin and spread out all over. He tried to pull himself together but found that he felt thin and wavy as he flew. The landscape beneath him looked almost like a crazy quilt of colors or a messy, colored scribble picture he had made. The sounds of birds and animals started loudly and then began to fade. For a brief period, it was totally quiet. The only sound he could hear was his own breathing. It was completely peaceful with the warm sun and bright colors. Looking at Newt, Ryan was shocked to notice how green he really looked in this light.

"This feels really weird. What's happening? Newt, why do you look so green," Ryan asked.

"Huh? Didn't realize it," he responded as if he had been sleeping.

"What's up, guys? Oh, not to worry. As we land on Puffy the Cloud, better known as Thunderhead, you'll cool off a bit and turn back to the water drop. For now, you are sort of like water vapor. This way humans can't see us travel. You know, Newt, you are really looking green," Curie replied. "Are you feeling ok?"

"Not really," Newt mumbled.

"You didn't swim through that green liquid near the shore to help Ryan with Bo did you," Albert asked.

"Not sure. Why," asked Newt while rubbing his tummy.

" Because, don't you remember Franky? He did and got really sick! He almost died! Old Alf had to give him special medicine and a soap bath to make him better," Albert said as he raised his head to look at Newt.

"Who's Franky," Ryan asked.

"Forgot about him. Gee, hope Alf is at the party so he can help me out. I do sort of feel sick," Newt sighed as he began to get worried.

"Oh, Franky was a field mouse who used to visit us when we were water drops years ago. He accidentally swam through green liquid stuff coming from a plastic bottle that had been thrown on the shore. I think the bottle said anti-freeze on it. Some human had discarded it like the others," Curie replied.

"Yes, if we are water drops, remember we soak up what we go through. In this case, I bet you got some of the green anti-freeze into you and you are getting sick," Vini warned Newt.

"Let's hurry and get Alf to help Newt before he gets worse," Louis shouted from the farthest color on the edge of the rainbow.

"I sure didn't know humans were so careless. I really hope we can fix things," Ryan sighed and held Newt's hand to comfort him on his way to the cloud. "Can't we go faster?"

"Nope. Only as fast as the sun will carry us. Won't be long now. Hold on, old buddy. We're almost there," Albert stated as he began to look worried as well.

Before they reached the top, they all started shouting for Alf as loud as they could. Luckily, Alf had heard that they may be coming to the cloud and he arrived early to set up for the party.

"What's wrong, fellas? I'm right here. Didn't think I'd forget did ya," Alf replied.

"Boy are we glad to see you," Ryan shouted. "Hello, again. You got to help Newt."

"Newt? What's wrong. You hurt," Alf shouted back as they reached the top.

"Ugh. Don't feel good," he replied, holding his tummy.

"Don't look good either, my boy. Why so green," Alf asked as he helped Newt from his color on the rainbow.

"He swam through green anti-freeze like Franky did. You got to save him! You got to," Albert pleaded to Alf.

"Is that all," Alf said, looking down at Newt.

"Newt. You are water, right," Alf asked.

"Yes," Newt muttered, holding his green tummy as it jiggled.

"You won't get as sick as Franky. You can simply pass down as rain and get cleaned by man in the water bathhouse. Franky was an animal and needed to get a soap bath to get clean. He also needed medicine since he couldn't just pass the green stuff through his tummy and out," said Alf, trying to comfort Newt.

"Oh, like we did with the sand," asked Louis.

"And the coal dust," asked Curie.

"Yep," Alf replied, patting Newt on the back. "Man's garbage does make water sick, but usually it is for a short time until they clean it. If they don't, then you really have something to worry about. Animals and plants need the water like Franky and the roots. If water is sick, they will make them sick, too."

"So, I'll be ok," Newt asked, raising his head.

"Just rest, and soon you'll feel better. You'll last until you rain down and get clean," Alf replied.

Newt made himself comfortable on a soft, puffy cushion of cloud and began to sleep.

"Are you sure he'll be ok," Curie asked Alf quietly. The rest of the group members were huddled around Newt to make him feel better.

"Well, I think so, but you'll need to cut the party short this time to get rained down, for his sake. If you take too long, I'm afraid he'll be in pretty bad shape," confided Alf to Curie with a word of caution.

"Come on Ryan, let's let him rest. You need to meet everyone and Puffy, too," Albert said, pulling at Ryan.

Just then, a face appeared in front of Ryan and the Eigenoids. The face was formed with clouds and seemed really fluffy and friendly. Ryan wasn't scared this time as it reminded him of funny faces he made with marshmallows. The eyebrows were thick and raised high above the eyes. Beneath a large, fat nose appeared a twisty mustache with pouty lips.

"Say, Fellas! And Lady! I missed you! Welcome aboard," replied the face with a smile.

"Ryan, meet Puffy the Cloud. He hosts our family parties," Albert said as he introduced Ryan.

"Pleased to meet you," Ryan said with a slight laugh.

"You can call me Puff for short, or my real nickname is Thunderhead. Less formal you know," Puffy replied. "Say, let Newt sleep. I'll keep him safe. You guys go ahead. The crew's been gathering for some time now. They have been waiting for their captains and the guest of honor."

"Ok. Let's get going," Albert replied, taking a hold of Ryan's hand and pulling him forward.

Ryan looked back at Newt who was cozy in a ball sleeping on the cloud. Puffy rolled a piece of cloud over him like a blanket and Newt began to snore. Rolling forward with Albert and the other Eigenoids, Ryan found it difficult to travel on the cloud. A couple of times, he pressed to hard with his foot and it went straight through the bottom of the cloud. They passed across a thin stretch of cloud and soon came to a bridge made of white puffy cloud. Ryan realized that Puffy could transform into any shape they needed to get across the sky. At one point he was a bridge, then a boat and then a path like a sidewalk. Curious to see what the party was, he kept going.

"Say, Thunderhead, why do they call you that and how do you keep changing," Ryan asked.

"Well, haven't you ever met a cloud? We always change. Sometimes humans look up at us and think we make shapes of things they recognize. I once had a human point to me and think I looked like a dragon. I tricked him and had some fun so I changed into a bunny rabbit before his friend could see me. We had a good laugh at that one," Puffy laughed, telling his story as his funny face appeared again.

He continued, "They call me Thunderhead because when we have parties, I grow big and tall. Usually the parties end up in rain storms with thunder and lightning."

Songs and laughter floated over a big hill in front of Ryan and the Eigenoids. They had made it to the party. Anxious to see what was going on, Ryan tried to climb up the hill that Puffy had made. Every time he sank his foot into the hill, it came right back. He could not climb upward. He just kept falling back down.

"Hey! What's the big idea? I thought you wanted us to go to the party," Ryan asked, looking puzzled.

The Eigenoids laughed and knew that Puffy had to make an entrance first as the host or he wouldn't let them pass. This was the rule he had made centuries ago, and never changed.

"Just wait one minute, youngster. I need to make an entrance and announce the guests," Puffy said, clearing his voice and raising the hill higher. "And now, Eigenoids of all ages, water and friends, the moment you've waited for, The Eigenoids of Long Past have returned with their hero, Ryan," Puffy shouted in a deep voice that shook the cloud and everything around them.

Slowly Puffy lowered the hill and Ryan couldn't believe his eyes. In front of him were hundreds of little Eigenoids old and young. He saw water drops like him and even hard ice like particles all dancing and cheering at them as they approached the mass of creatures. Albert, Curie, Vini, Louis and Alf all joined hands and bowed in honor as everyone stopped singing and dancing to look at them. Suddenly, Ryan stepped forward to get a better view and the crowd before him cheered loudly and jumped up and down with praises.

"Why are they so happy to see me," Ryan whispered to Albert.

"Alf said he told them you were a hero to protect us from humans. They may even think you are going after King Odious. Just nod and smile. Wave," Albert replied.

"What," yelled Ryan.

"Shhhhhhhhh," urged Curie, grabbing Ryan's arm and covering his mouth. "Don't spoil the party. Remember, Newt needs this so we can rain down and he can get better."

Ryan did as he was asked. He nodded and waved. As he lowered his arm, Alf stepped forward, raised his hands and began to speak. A silence passed over the crowd again.

"My fellow Eigenoids, water and guests - I am pleased to see all of you here. We cannot stay for fear of King Odious, as we are not yet ready for battle. Let's have a quick coming together and celebrate the return of the Eigenoids of Long Past as they have become to be called. We welcome our new hero and friend, Ryan as well. Three cheers—Hip Poya! Hip Poya!, Hip Poya," Alf cheered as they raised a glass in a toast to Ryan.

"Let's dance. Let's dance," Vini shouted.

Suddenly, everyone was forming lines and started to dance. Music came sounding over the cloud and Puffy began making drum sounds to keep beat. They all did the same dance in lines. First they moved to the right, then to the left. Next, they went to the rear and turned around twice. Lastly, they moved forward, kicked their feet and clapped their hands. The dance looked like something he had seen his parent's do at a cousin's wedding. Ryan couldn't believe his eyes. Something funny began to happen, the longer they watched everyone dance. Ryan began to get colder and his shape became more prominent like a true water drop. Up till now, he had been mis-shaped from his travel up the rainbow. He had not noticed it before.

"Um—Curie, how does it rain? And, is there a party like this every time it rains," Ryan asked.

"Well, if we're lucky, either too many show up and we get over-crowded so some abandon ship and they turn to rain. If not, maybe a fight will break out and a brawl starts and some get knocked off, causing it to rain. It just depends," Curie replied, clapping her hands to the beat.

"Haven't you ever heard of the greatest party, ever," Vini asked Ryan.

"Uh - no. Remember, this is my first one," Ryan replied.

"Come now, boy. Seriously. You haven't heard of the big one," Puffy stopped keeping beat to tell his story to Ryan. "Someone keep beat while I tell the story to the newcomer."

"I got it," a voice shouted from the crowd below.

Puffy formed a big drum and drum sticks for the little Eigenoid to keep playing. He picked up the sticks and began playing without missing a beat.

"The big one is the best party ever in history. We try to repeat it, but the One stops us. We have been forbidden to ever have a party that big again. Only once in history were we allowed and boy it was a good one, too. You see, I am the last being before you get to the Outer Realm. I didn't know any better early on, and one time I was convinced to have a large party. I invited all of the Eigenoids, and all forms of moisture to the party. The problem was that I didn't space them out on arrival and departure and I had too many here. The One who controls all realms allowed me to have a party, not sure why, but just did. A fight broke out and we got too noisy and rowdy. By the time we ended, we had rained for forty days and nights. We damaged the Animal Kingdom and the Inner Realm so bad that the One had to repair it and rebuild half or all of what we destroyed. Ever since, we have been limited to how many we could have and for how long we can party. We always try to beat it, but the One stops us before we damage stuff again," Puffy said, sharing his story.

"Wow, I never heard it like that! I did hear of the big one, I guess. Only, I heard it a bit different with a man named Noah and a flood," Ryan replied.

Puffy went back to keeping beat. As Ryan observed, he noticed several Eigenoids and water drops starting in on a different dance. Some would climb up on a hill and jump down. As they jumped down, they would say mean things to jar at each other. These negative statements generated a lot of warm air. When the Eigenoids or water would climb upward or jump up to the top of the hill, they would counteract the negative with positive statements and happy thoughts. It looked like a game at first. Ryan thought it was really odd. Soon, the entire crowd quit dancing and began following in the weird game. Before long, it didn't seem like a game. Some decided to push others off of the hill. Some decided to pull at each other, and as expected, a fight began to break out.

"Here we go again. I'm sorry Ryan. Get ready, the Animal Kingdom is going to try to stop them because I can never manage them," Puffy exclaimed.

Just then Vini laughed and pointed towards the ground way beneath them. "It is going to get hot and you will have to be ready to jump out of the way."

"Why? What's happening," Ryan asked as he started looking down.

"Someone must have insulted someone below and they are coming up to fight," Puffy shouted.

"You see, Ryan, the negative comments, negative energy, passed through things and made it to the ground. The ground doesn't like it and passes it up here by way of a lightning bolt to join the fight. Lightning bolts are hotter than the sun, so you must try to avoid them if they reach clear up here. As soon as there are too many up here, Thunderhead over here will make us jump out. That is rain," Curie tried to explain to Ryan who was peering over the edge of Puffy.

"Oh," Ryan said stretching way over the side to see if he could see anyone trying to come up.

Suddenly, Albert and Vini jumped high in the air and rolled to their right to avoid a bright flash of light.

"Well, let's get this started," two voices shouted as two Eigenoids jumped out from the light.

Their entrance and voices were so loud that it sent a shock wave rumbling past Ryan so fast that he could hardly catch his breath. Ryan quickly surmised that this was the thunder in a rainstorm. Ryan realized that this was the thunder and lightning he had always seen and heard in the clouds. He then understood that he didn't need to fear storms anymore.

"Watch out! Here we go! It's working! Look," shouted Curie as she pointed to a big ravine opening up between the Eigenoids and the crowd.

"Well, got to say good bye my friends. Here comes Newt, too. Just too many of you up here and I feel too heavy and the fighting game is getting out of hand as usual. Got to let you go," Puffy replied as he spread his big, fluffy arms wide and they began to fall.

"Wee," shouted Albert as he started to fall.

"Hey! This is weird! What will we land on?" Ryan shouted.

"Don't worry. We're still over the river. We can swim. We're water, remember," Albert shouted back.

"Grab my hand," Curie shouted and grabbed Ryan's arm to help him fall. "Feeling better Newt?"

"A little. I will be back to myself soon, I hope. Still feeling green, though," Newt replied, stretching his arms as he woke from his nap.

Together they all started to fall. As Ryan fell, he saw other Eigenoids and water drops waving good bye and giving hugs to each other. He glanced up and saw Thunderhead, Puffy the Cloud, whom now looked dark blue from all of the water inside of him, give a smile and wink his eye. He raised his puffy hand that had formed and waved farewell to his new friend.

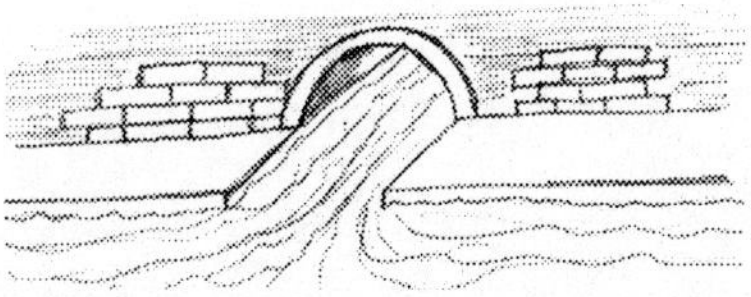

Chapter 17: Bath Time

"Say, Albert? Got the map," Louis asked Albert. "Are we in the same river or stream as we were before? I don't want to hit the green stuff below like Newt did."

"Nope. Map is in Ryan's pack. Got it Rye," Albert shouted as they fell closer to the stream below.

"It's right here. I'll get it," Ryan replied, swinging his pack in front of him and pulling out the map.

Just then, Ryan hit the stream in a big splash almost loosing the map and his pack. He hadn't noticed how fast they had been falling and misjudged his landing.

"Be careful, old boy. Don't want to lose it again," Albert shouted over to Ryan. "Swim over to me so I can read it.

As Ryan swam, he began to read a bit of the journal back to Albert.

"It says, when we come to an oak tree stump, we are to follow the path to the right over the rapids to the water plant," Ryan said as he swam swinging the map in the air with one hand.

"That's good. Almost there now! What else does it say," asked Albert who was swimming towards Ryan.

Together they looked at the map. By the time they had things figured out, they were all at the stump. Looking up, Ryan saw fast water going to the right in the direction they were to travel. He was scared, but he knew that they had to follow the map. A couple of times so far, they had gotten off track and had some scary troubles. He didn't want anymore problems, but was ready to go home. Together the Eigenoids and Ryan joined hands and formed a ring to stay together. They decided it was best to follow the map and brave the rapids head-on.

The water started getting really fast and bouncing them all over the place. It became really hard to keep holding hands. Struggling to keep his eyes above the water, Ryan soon found himself submersed up and down in a roller coaster motion through high waves and crushing rocks. As soon as then passed over the rocks, the stream calmed down and the ride was smooth again. Ryan decided to try and look around again. He was concerned for Newt and decided to try to point out pretty flowers to cheer him up.

"Hey, look at that flower. You see it, the pink one, there," Ryan said as he motioned to Newt.

Newt still had a green look to him and didn't seem to be getting better.

"Are we almost there? Newt doesn't look too good, guys. I'm tired, too. My Mom is probably worried," Ryan began to ask a lot of questions again.

"Almost. It should be coming up any minute. Here we go. Jump into that grate. It leads straight to the water plant or bathhouse for water. We can all get cleaned up," Vini said as he jumped straight down into a grate on the shore.

Just as before, one by one, they followed the leader into another strange land. Ryan didn't know what to expect, but he knew that Newt needed to get clean. Curie also knew that Newt might not make it back after this trip if they didn't find the chemical stripper right away. She pulled at Newt's wrinkled, shrinking hand to pull him along.

"Newt. Don't give up. We can make it. It is just a bit farther. You have to do it. Newt," Curie cried for help as Newt started to collapse.

"Don't think I can," Newt replied. "Feeling really wrinkled and tired."

Ryan saw Newt and Curie struggling and came to help him. "Lean on me, Newt. I am strong. I can carry you if I need to," Ryan said.

"No you can't. You are no bigger than me," Newt replied, smiling at the warm gesture from his friend.

"Here. Use this. Climb on, Newt," Vini said, rushing to their aid.

Vini had fashioned together a couple of grass blades into sort of a splint-like pad for Newt to ride on. Newt climbed onto it and lay down. It took both Ryan and Vini to carry Newt by pulling at one end of the grass blades.

"Thanks, Vin. You really came through," Newt replied with a sigh and shut his eyes.

"Let's hurry guys, I can see the entrance. Hold on, old buddy," Albert said as he grabbed the grass near Ryan to help.

Together they managed to get to the entrance of the Chemical Stripping station. With a warning to Ryan to stay together, they all went in pulling Newt on his grass blanket. They told Ryan that they needed a specific tunnel to save Newt. One tunnel lead to a real stinky place that took forever to get cleaned. The other was a shortcut they had found into the Chemical Stripper to remove the bad chemicals. It was Newt's only hope to survive. Once inside, Ryan saw all kinds of shiny metal tables and tanks. Together they ended up on another pipe that was shiny and clean. Following the flow of other water drops, they found themselves getting dumped into a large tank. It took all of their strength to hold poor Newt's head up while they began to float in a circular motion around the tank.

"This is fun, Newt. Wake up. You'll feel better in a minute," Ryan urged him as he started to giggle.

"Oh, Newt. You got to wake up! You just got to," Curie cried. She began to be really quiet.

"Albert, you don't think, he's," Louis said softly as he started to cry.

"No. Not my Newt. Not my pal," cried Albert as he grabbed Newt's hand and put his head down.

"What? I thought you said he'd be Ok," Ryan said, looking at the wrinkled, lifeless-looking water drop.

Newt was beginning to start to change into his old self, an Eigenoid. They began to hum in great sorrow for their fallen friend.

"What's happening? Why is he changing back? Wake up Newt, Wake up," Ryan began to shake Newt as violently as he could to try to wake him.

Newt began to groan a bit, but could not speak, for he was too weak. He could not even lift his head or open his eyes. Slowly his color started to fade to gray and the green cast was vanishing before their eyes. They were so consumed with grief that they didn't see they had floated under a long pipe funnel hanging overhead.

"Guys, quick, over here. Bring Newt over here. Here is the tube we need! Wait for it. Wait for it. NOW," Vini yelled at the top of his voice.

As if he had commanded it to do so, a large pipe went down into the water and a funny looking chemical squirted out under the water. They had managed to get Newt right next to the tube when it hit the water. The funny pink foam that came out under the water floated up and all around them. The heaviest concentration was all over Newt. The pink foam was a chemical used to remove bad chemicals from the water. The foam bubbled up and soon enveloped them to where they couldn't see each other or Newt.

Suddenly, a bright light flashed inside of the foam where Newt had been. Ryan felt his hopes soar as he heard Newt's faint voice.

"Took long enough, don't you think," came a shrill voice that sounded scratchy.

It was Newt! He had survived and was returned back to a water drop. Although he had started to change into an Eigenoid and almost die, there was still enough energy left in him as a water drop that the chemicals removed the bad green antifreeze in the nick of time.

"NEWT," they all shouted. "You're alive!"

"We thought you had died and were going to see the One," Louis cried with joy.

"Let me see you old pal. Good to have you back," Albert reached through the foam trying to pat it down for visibility.

"Sorry for the scare. Thought I was a goner, too," replied Newt, stretching his hand out to grab Albert for support.

"Yah. Glad to hear you Newt. Don't know what we'd do without you. Don't like to be scared like that, that's for certain," Ryan said, crying for joy as they all tried to hug Newt.

"Now don't squish me! I still feel funny," Newt said as he tried to get away.

"Come on now, boy. You know I get a hug and maybe a kiss," Curie swam towards him. "We are all in this together. No leaving early. I love you guys!"

"We owe it all to Vini," Louis said with a smile as he patted Vini on his back.

"Hey," Vini bowed his head a bit. "Yeah, took me some time to read where the pipe came down. Glad to have you back with us. Wouldn't want to have to build something to carry you home in."

"Vini," Curie scolded him in shock.

"Just kidding. Love ya too, old friend. Just don't cut it so close anymore and look where you swim," Vini replied, laughing and hugging Newt.

"Look, the foam is almost gone! What happens next," Ryan asked, pointing to the foam lowering and dissolving into the water.

"Well, that felt great! I feel much better now," Newt said as he stretched his arms and kicked his legs.

He began swimming around very fast to try to kick the foam down. As he did, Ryan noticed that each Eigenoid started to shine and sparkle. He even began to feel slick and wiggly inside.

"Your color! It's back! You're a green cast again, but not too much green," Curie said, pointing to Newt.

"Well, Ryan, it's off to the reservoir. You see, we've been bathed and chemicals added to us by the foam.

Human's can drink us if they need to. We don't want them to, but they can drink the regular drops. From the reservoir, we go to houses and get used," Albert said in a matter-of-fact teacher's voice.

"You mean, that's it," Ryan asked.

As fast as the water had started to spin, it was now calm and clear. Ryan could see clear to the bottom of the tank. Everything was a shiny steel color.

"What chemicals were added? I didn't feel anything. I do feel a bit heavier like I gained weight," Ryan continued.

"Oh, they added fluoride and water softener stuff. You gain weight, but you're clean," Vini replied.

"We want to go to the reservoir, right," Vini asked as he pointed to a pipe with a sign overhead. "That says 'General population,' NOT reservoir!"

"Quick! Swim as fast as you can. We have to escape the undertow. It will pull us in. Hurry," Albert screamed.

"I can't," Curie went under the water.

Next went Ryan and then the rest of the Eigenoids. The water current pulled them under and into a long dark pipe. They missed the exit to the reservoir and were on their way to someone's house.

Gasping for air and sputtering Ryan managed to get his head back above the water. "Help, guys," he muttered.

One by one they popped their head above the water, too.

"Oh no," Albert yelled. "Give me the pack! Ryan, say the words, quick!"

"What? I can't hear you over the roar of the waves," Ryan yelled back.

"Here," Vini said, pulling Ryan to a valve that was sticking into the water. "Everyone, over here!"

Together, all the Eigenoids and Ryan managed to climb up on the valve hanging into the water.

"It sure is getting dark the farther we get from the water bathhouse. Where are we? What is General Population," Ryan asked.

"Get the journal. Quick, Ryan. Say the words before we get sucked out," Albert shouted as he grabbed at the pack on Ryan's back.

"What words? What's going on," Ryan asked.

"You need to change us back before someone turns on their faucet and we come out. When they turn the faucet on in a sink, we get sucked out with the water flow. We don't want to be drank!" Vini interrupted, pushing the journal to Ryan.

'How do I change us back? What words," Ryan said, looking shocked.

"Here, the words. You know, the words to go back," Albert pointed into the journal, holding Ryan's flashlight on the journal.

"Ok. Here goes," Ryan started.

"Hurry up will ya," Louis shouted, barely hanging onto the valve and kicking his feet in the water.

"Ok. Ok," Ryan started speaking:

Now that I've learned to see, please send me back to where I should be.

Suddenly, they all rose up into the air above the water. They all started spinning, and a mass of colored light engulfed them. Ryan could no longer see or hear anything, yet, he felt himself changing and moving.

Chapter 18: Eyes Wide Open

As quickly as the bright colors appeared, they faded to black. Ryan rubbed his eyes to try to see where he was and what had happened.

"Uh, guys? Where are you? What happened," Ryan said, slowly focusing on his hand.

That's right. His hand, his real hand. Looking around, Ryan found himself sitting on the mat in his room as if he had never left. The box was in front of him and it was opened. He heard the Eigenoids laughing. He was a real boy again. He had been changed back and put right back into his room as if he had never left.

"Ryan, are you done eating," Ryan heard his mother say as she came down the hall.

"Where's my boy," Ryan's dad shouted, coming in the door from the garage.

"What," Ryan thought, saying to himself. "Finished eating? Dad is just coming home? How can that be. I was gone so long. I thought they'd miss me for sure. Too COOL!"

"Ryan, put us back in the box. Your Mom's coming. Hurry up," Albert yelled for Ryan.

"Oh, guys, how did you," Ryan said, approaching the box and wanting to talk.

He suddenly heard his mother start to rattle the doorknob.

"Honey, can you help me here," Dad's voice called to Mother for help. "Got groceries while I was out, too."

"Coming," Ryan's Mom replied and left the doorway to go help Ryan's dad.

"Whew, that was close. Come on Ryan. We'll catch up later. What a first round my boy. Best one in a while," Albert said.

"But, how come they don't know I was gone. It is like I never left," Ryan asked quickly.

"They don't. You see, in our world when they shrank the Eigenoids and the Inner realm, time slowed. One Eigen moment in our time is equivalent to only a nanosecond in yours. Time basically stands almost still in your world as compared to ours," Newt responded.

"Yah, you'll do for a keeper alright," Vini said with a smile and wink of his eye.

"I owe ya, Rye. Really. Thanks. Let's do it again, not this, but again, you know," Newt said as he put his eyeglass back in his pocket and turned to go to the box.

"Curie, are you ok," Ryan asked as he saw her bow her head.

"Just have a spec in my eye," Curie said, wiping away a tear. "Take care until we see you again. Be a good boy. We'll miss you."

They all joined hands and spun into their light of colors. The lighted ball went into the box and it closed. Ryan quickly waved good bye to them and closed the latch. As he did, the latch disappeared and the box looked as it did before. He quickly put the box in the hiding place along with the pack and journal. He couldn't wait to tell his dad about his quest for the start of the water cycle, but then he remembered what his Pa-Pa had said. He realized that his dad and mom wouldn't believe him. They didn't even realize he had gone. Ryan decided to act as if he had been in his room the whole time.

"Mom, can I go to Scotty's house," Ryan asked, opening his door.

"Nope. How about if he comes over here again tonight," Ryan's Mom asked him with a smile.

"Why," Ryan asked. "I thought he was staying at his Aunt's house."

"Nope, his Mommy called and said they postponed their trip. They had to go somewhere and asked if Scotty could stay tonight while they were gone. I said it was ok. He'll be over soon," said his mother, smiling and patting Ryan's head.

"Cool. I've got a lot to tell him," Ryan said, jumping up and down.

"Lots about what," Ryan's dad asked, looking inquisitively at Ryan over his sunglasses.

"Oh, nothing. Um, just about my video game. I scored really high," Ryan replied as quickly as he could with anything that would change the conversation. "When do I go to Pa-Pa's again?"

"Not sure," replied Ryan's mother looking perplexed at Ryan. "Guess you had fun, huh?"

"Yep. I just want to finish the attic like I promised. So when is Scotty coming over?" Ryan tried to change the subject again as he reached to help his dad with groceries.

"Thanks, my boy. Let's put them away for Mom before scotty gets here." Dad replied with a smile.

Before long, Scotty was in Ryan's room with him and Ryan was trying to explain all about the Eigneoids. He described the different places they had been and how he transformed and what the world looked like from the Inner Realm. Ryan planned to show him the box and the creatures when they were interrupted for dinner. Ryan had managed to pull out the box, but not the journal, when his Mother called them for dinner.

"Ryan, don't bring that silly box. Let's play galaxy wars after dinner. I don't like pretending stuff like that box thing. It was fun for your Grandpa to not upset him, but get real. Little creatures," Scotty said as they washed up for dinner. "Say, don't forget, on Wednesday Billy Paxton is pitching and we have to practice so we can beat his team."

"They are real," Ryan said with hurt feelings. "Don't worry about the ball game coming up. We'll practice tonight with my dad. He's home tonight."

Ryan and Scotty were on the same little league team and had a very important game coming up for their season. Billy Paxton was a grade ahead of them and always picked on Scotty. Ryan, who had loved baseball since he was two years old, was one of the best players on his team. He was scheduled to pitch on his team for the next game. Scotty realized that he had upset Ryan and was trying to change the subject as he finished drying his hands and started down the hallway. Disappointed and sad, Ryan went to his room and hid the box. When he put it away, he heard a small giggle coming from inside.

"We believe, don't we," Ryan said with a smile and then tucked the box away for safekeeping.

He went down the hall to the kitchen and heard Scotty laughing about the box with his dad.

"It was real," Ryan said as he hung his head.

"Ok, now that's enough boys. Dad, you too. Ryan, I know you had fun in your room today. Let's forget about it for now. Scotty's here and you can play things he likes, ok," Mom said as she sat a plate of hotdogs on the table in front of the two boys.

Ryan's mom smiled at Ryan and winked. Not sure if she knew or not, Ryan decided to keep it a secret from now on. He realized that he was just like his Pa-Pa. Scotty didn't believe and it was up to Ryan to save the Eigenoids. Maybe he could rescue their kingdom and save them from King Odious. Then they could come to his world and everyone would believe him. Just maybe he could be a hero for them.

Smiling to himself, Ryan agreed and decided to enjoy his hotdog. After all, swimming, fighting off ants and roots, flying and transforming will work up an appetite.

WORD FIND

S	T	L	I	G	H	T	E	N	I	N	G
B	H	U	A	V	J	M	R	A	M	O	E
M	U	C	R	E	I	G	E	N	O	I	D
A	N	R	R	O	B	C	I	P	A	T	I
N	D	E	P	O	H	E	V	S	S	A	K
L	E	V	A	P	O	R	A	T	E	M	I
M	R	I	A	Q	E	T	A	A	Y	R	N
R	H	C	A	Q	U	L	S	L	L	O	F
E	E	E	A	Y	A	A	M	A	M	F	I
C	A	Y	E	G	O	Q	B	C	B	S	L
Y	D	A	M	O	M	U	O	T	I	N	T
C	R	I	M	T	J	I	M	I	M	A	R
L	T	L	E	E	C	F	T	T	Y	R	A
E	Q	U	E	S	T	E	Y	E	H	T	T
B	U	R	P	Y	G	R	E	A	L	M	E

WORDS:

AQUA
AQUIFER
BURPY
CREVICE
EIGENOID
EVAPORATE
INFILTRATE
LIGHTENING

QUEST
REALM
RECYCLE
ROOTS
STALACTITE
STALAGMITE
THUNDERHEAD
TRANSFORMATION

NOTES

WORD FIND ANSWER KEY

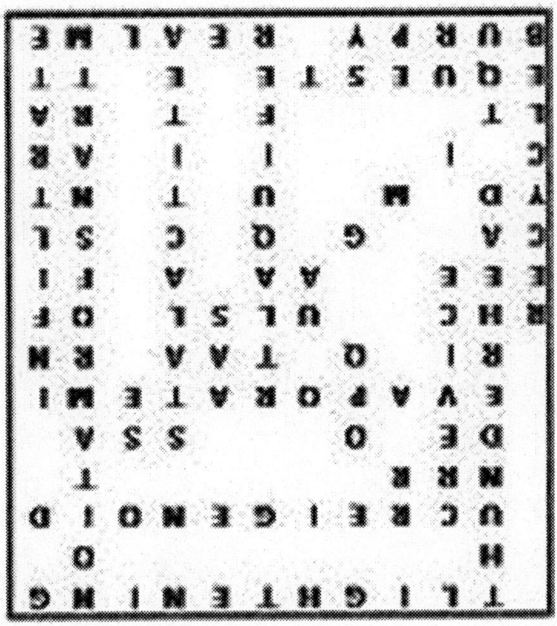